The Yshan Kings Saga

by

Michael Davies

The Yshan Kings Saga

For information address: info@mickiedaltonfoundation.com

First Published in 2020 in Australia

ISBN: 978-0-6485470-8-2

FIRST PRINTED IN AUSTRALIA

Published by The Mickie Dalton Foundation
NSW
Australia

www.mickiedaltonfoundation.com

Other Books by Michael Davies

The Nightmares of God
The Janus Conspiracy
A Friendly Killing
Dreamkill
Ready, Steady, KILL!
Accounts of a Killing
Helix Dreams
Helix – The Second Renaissance

For the Young Adults (12-18)
The Many Worlds of Mickie Dalton
The Many Galaxies of Mickie Dalton
The Many Universes of Mickie Dalton
The Strange World of Mark and Anna

For the 8-11 Age Group
The Julie Malloy Gang and the Smugglers
The Quest for the Locket
The Secret of Yuri Kirilenko
The United Nations and the Extra-Terrestrial
The Secret of Charlotte's Cello
The Mysterious Recorder and the Door to Elsewhere
The Red Fog of Time
Prisoners of the Picture
A Step Into the Past
What Can't be Seen can Exist
How I Spent My Evening

For the 3-5 Age Group
Mary's World

And in non-fiction
The Business School Approach to Writing Your Novel

Part One

The Star of the Yshan Kings

Chapter 1 - The New Arrivals

Josh Bradshaw was the first to see the new arrivals.

He was working with his Sensei Master on the front lawn of the school where he had a regular morning work-out and the master had just shown him in slow motion the way to drive his fist at the opponent's chest, when Josh saw the big, black four-wheel drive vehicle stop at the gates. He took a short breather to watch as two children and two adults got out. He thought the children might be his own age, perhaps thirteen, and they were both tall and good-looking, moving with self-confidence and athletic grace.

The adults got out first, one on each side of the vehicle and looked around before the other two climbed out and they walked up the path to the school entrance.

"Do you want to stop there, Josh?" asked his teacher. "It looks like you're interested in the new students!"

"Thank you, Master," Josh replied and they bowed to each other before the teacher went to his car to go back to his Karate Academy and Josh went to take a shower and get ready for classes.

Charlie Foster had also seen the arrivals as she rode up on her mountain bike. She stopped a few metres from the big car as she took her helmet off and shook out her long hair.

"Curious," she said to herself as she watched the adults then the children climb out. "What strange parents! They look like they were checking out the scene before they let the kids out!"

She waited until the four newcomers had entered the school then wheeled her bike to the sheds at the side. She saw Josh heading in as well and decided that they and Henry should talk about the interesting new students as soon as they could.

As they reached the front door, she was about to speak to Josh when she realised somebody else was standing there, watching the group walk down to the Principal's office.

"Good morning, Miss Hickey," said Josh and was echoed by Charlie. They both liked the new teacher, Jennifer Hickey who had arrived last term. She was very pretty and always cheerful and she had taken over teaching sports, even coaching the school's soccer team. Josh had been highly impressed by how fast she seemed to move and how strong she was.

"Good morning, Josh, Charlie," the teacher replied. Charlie thought she seemed preoccupied as she watched the group enter the Principal's office.

"Do we know who they are?" asked Charlie and Miss Hickey nodded.

"They've just moved into the region," she said. "I think they're from Sydney."

"I hope we get to meet them soon," said Josh. "They both look like they're good at sport."

"I'm sure they are," said the teacher. "But children, be a little careful. Don't get too close to them."

With that, she walked away.

"What a very strange thing to say," Josh said. "I wonder what she meant?"

"No idea," Charlie replied. "Hey, we're going to be late for classes."

* * *

When Henry met the new people, he didn't just sit back and watch them. That wasn't Henry's way. Although he was only nine years old, two years younger than Charlie and four years younger than Josh, he was a friendly, social boy with no shortage of self-confidence. As soon as he saw the newcomers sitting at a table during the lunch break, he walked up to them.

"G'day!" he said, cheerfully. "Welcome to Macleay Public School! My name's Henry Jackson!"

For a moment, the pair sitting opposite him looked confused. Henry actually thought briefly that the girl looked angry and wondered why.

"Oh.... Hello!" the boy finally said. "My name is Kyle and this is my sister, Sophie."

"You look very much alike," Henry said. "Are you twins?"

"Yes, we are," Kyle replied.

At that moment, Charlie and Josh arrived and also took seats.

"Hi!" said Charlie. "I'm Charlie. It's supposed to be Charlotte, but I hate that silly name."

"And I'm Josh. Short for Joshua."

"It's good to meet you," said Kyle. "Being new at a strange school is rather difficult."

"Where are you from?" asked Charlie.

Finally Sophie spoke. "We're from Sydney," she said. "Our parents are here to work on the Kempsey by-pass of the Pacific Highway. They're both engineers."

She sounded quite cool and distant, Henry thought, but he put that down to her being shy. He looked around the hall and saw Miss Hickey watching the group and wondered why she looked so attentive. She seemed to be looking at them with great concern.

"I saw you working at combat skills," said Kyle with a friendly grin at Josh. "I do that stuff too!"

"Oh great!" Josh replied. "Would you like a work-out sometime?"

"I really would!" Kyle replied and the two boys obviously became friends.

"Well, I ride horses," said Charlie. "Do either of you?"

For the first time, Sophie seemed to warm up. "Oh yes!" she replied with a smile. "We both ride a lot at home. Do you have a stable?"

"Yes!" said Charlie with delight. "My parents breed stock horses at our farm. You're welcome to come along at the weekend."

"You look a bit older than most people here," said Josh. "I'm thirteen, but I'll be going to High School next year."

"We're eleven," replied Kyle. "But I know we look older than that. Our parents are both tall and I suppose we're the same."

Henry had gone quiet. He seemed to be looking intently at both Sophie and Kyle but although Kyle didn't seem to notice, Sophie was staring back and her face was cold and expressionless.

"And what do you do, little boy?" she asked. "I suppose you just play with silly toys?"

There was a moment of silence round the table before Henry broke it.

"I play chess," he said. "And I can beat anyone."

"Not me," Sophie replied.

"Henry plays regional tournaments," said Charlie, placing an affectionate hand on Henry's shoulder. "And he won the school tournament this year."

"And I challenge you," said Henry.

"And I'll beat you," said Sophie.

All of them recognised the strange tension between Henry and Sophie. Kyle looked disturbed.

"I'll meet you at the end of school in the hall," said Josh, breaking the strained atmosphere. "We've got practice mats there. I'm sure one of the teachers will give us permission."

Kyle seemed relieved at that. "You bet!" he replied.

And the five children broke up to go to their classes.

Chapter 2 - Getting Acquainted

Josh was the first to get to the hall as the final bell sounded and he had changed into his Karate clothes as Kyle entered the changing room. They grinned at each other as if they'd been friends for years.

They sat and talked a bit as Kyle changed. Josh decided that Kyle looked extremely strong and fit.

"That's an interesting thing you have round your neck," he said. "What is it?"

As far as Josh could tell, it was a gold disc but it had a strangely bright spot in the middle of it.

"Oh, just a family thing," Kyle replied carelessly and tucked it under his shirt. Josh decided to ignore it.

"How long have you been studying Karate?" he asked.

"As long as I can remember," said Kyle.

"What, since you were a baby?" Josh was astonished.

"Well, I really can't remember my first lessons. It seems to me I've always been training."

"That's weird!"

"It's traditional with my family," Kyle said and he seemed a little embarrassed. "C'mon, let's get to the hall."

Ten minutes later, Josh had learned just how good Kyle was. The new boy had ferocious speed and reflexes that left Josh feeling like a baby next to him. Try as he might, Josh couldn't land a single blow on Kyle who seemed to skip away like a shadow and return with a punch or chop that if they had landed with real force, would have injured Josh severely.

Eventually, it was Kyle who ended the work-out. Looking as if he had just walked a few yards, showing no fatigue and no breathlessness at all, he backed away, holding his hands up at Josh.

The two boys bowed at each other and made for the showers.

"You've had amazing teachers!" Josh said as they were changing back into street clothes.

"The very best," agreed Kyle. "Like I said, it's a form of tradition with my family."

"You must be a Black Belt at least!"

Kyle shook his head. "We don't have those grades," he said. "But I'm at the top back home, I know that. In my family, we regard it as a survival factor."

"Survival?" Josh was intrigued and puzzled. "Are you in danger for some reason?"

"Always," Kyle said. "Anyway, Sophie will be waiting and my parents will have arrived with the car."

The boys walked out to the front of the school where Sophie and Charlie were standing and talking about horse riding. Henry was not to be seen. As they arrived, the black vehicle was waiting, the parents got out and came up to them and spoke directly to the twins.

"You should not be outside," the father said. "You know you must always stay in cover."

Neither Kyle nor Sophie replied but let themselves be led to the car and climbed in, followed by the two adults. The windows were darkened so that Josh and Charlie couldn't see in, but they waved as the car moved away.

"That's just weird," said Charlie, watching it drive up the road.

"What is?"

"The parents," said Charlie. "The way they spoke, it felt more like they were servants, not parents."

"And Sophie and Kyle didn't introduce them to us, either."

"Almost as if we're not supposed to talk to them," said Charlie.

"There's something very strange about them," agreed Josh and he told her about Kyle's extraordinary skills at Karate.

"It'll be interesting to see how Sophie rides a horse," said Charlie. "After what you've told me, I'll bet she's a really great rider."

"I'm even more interested to see how she plays chess against Henry. If she's as good at that as Kyle is at Karate, this could be a great match."

"But I don't think she'll like it at all if Henry beats her," replied Charlie.

"Somehow I think you're right," said Josh and they split up to go home.

* * *

The chess match took place the following lunchtime. Henry walked up to where the twins were sitting alone at a table and placed the chessboard in front of Sophie, followed by the box of chess pieces.

"This is the challenge," he said firmly.

At that moment, they were joined by Charlie and Josh.

"This is the battle of the Grand Masters, is it?" said Charlie with a wide grin, but the others didn't respond the same way. Kyle looked worried. Sophie glared at Henry as if he was irritating her, but she opened the chess board anyway and began laying out the pieces. Henry also placed chessmen on the board then took a black and a white pawn, hid them under the table as he switched them around in his hands before holding out his clenched fists.

"Choose," he said.

Sophie touched one fist with an extended finger as if reluctant to touch Henry at all. He opened his hand to reveal a black pawn and he replaced both pawns on the board.

"White starts," he said and moved a pawn out in front of a Knight.

Sophie smiled with a cold expression and moved the opposite pawn out the same way.

Kyle murmured softly to Charlie and Josh, "She's a really good player and she hates losing."

Charlie grinned. "My money's on Henry!"

A moment later, Kyle watched the board and whispered, "Oh-oh, Henry's played the two Knights opening."

For the next twenty minutes, nobody spoke another word as the battle continued on the board. Josh was watching Sophie and he decided that she was showing signs of anxiety as Henry slowly took control and removed some of her major pieces.

The end came suddenly as Henry moved his Bishop out from the back row and sat back.

"Checkmate," he said softly.

Sophie didn't move, but stared at the board, her face white. Josh thought she looked like she was in shock.

"Well done, Henry!" said Kyle. "It's been a while since Sophie lost a match!"

"It's the best fight I've had in a long time," said Henry with a light smile. "Thank you, Sophie, I hope we can do that again sometime soon."

But Sophie stood up sharply, her chair falling backward with a crash.

"I hate you!" she said, picked up her King and threw it hard at Henry, straight at his face. If it had hit him, it could have caused serious damage, but Kyle moved so quickly, the others didn't have time to react. He moved over to Henry, stuck out his hand and caught the flying chess piece just a centimetre from the small boy's face.

In dead silence, Kyle replaced the King on the board and looked up at his sister. His face was cold.

"Sophie, you'd better get to your class," he said.

She turned away without speaking and strode away.

"I'm sorry," Kyle said after she had gone. "She's not used to losing."

"But why does she seem to hate Henry so much?" asked Charlie, almost in tears. "There's just no reason for that behaviour!"

"Kyle, I've never seen anyone move so fast," said Henry. "How did you do that?"

"Like I told Josh yesterday, I've been in training like this since I was a baby," Kyle said. "And I'm blessed with fast reflexes, I suppose."

"I'll say!" said Josh. "Can you teach me to move like that?"

Kyle grinned, at last losing his worried expression. "I don't know," he said. "But let's have another Karate workout this afternoon. Charlie, can we still come riding at the weekend?"

"I suppose so," replied Charlie. "But you'd better keep your sister under control!"

"I promise," said Kyle.

"And I'm not a horse person," said Henry. "I won't be there!"

Laughing as if they'd been friends for years, the group went to their classes. As they walked, Charlie saw Miss Hickey watching them all carefully.

Chapter 3 – The Mystery Deepens

Josh was already at the horse farm when the twins arrived. He loved visiting there, the fresh air, the horses in their paddocks and the beautifully maintained white fences along the driveways always seemed to lift his spirits.

He was also a great fan of Charlie's parents and spent as much time there as he could, rather than at his own home where life was nowhere near as pleasant.

They were all standing on the patio at the front of the house when the large black vehicle arrived. The twins climbed out without their parents and walked up to the house while the car drove off again immediately.

"Hello, you must be Kyle and Sophie!" said Charlie's mother. "I'm Alanna, welcome to our place."

Kyle grinned cheerfully, obviously feeling the friendship, but Sophie merely nodded her head and said "Hello" in almost a whisper. Alanna looked curiously at her while Charlie's father introduced himself.

"I'm Greg," he said. "And I'm a really bad actor!"

The kids all laughed, even Sophie smiled.

"Dad's fooling you," said Charlie. "I know he runs this beautiful farm but sometimes he gets a part in a play down in Sydney and he's away for a few weeks! He's trying out for a movie part next week!"

"That was strange, your parents driving off like that," said Alanna. "Why didn't they want to come in and meet everybody?"

Kyle looked uncomfortable. "I'm really sorry about that," he said. "They're just not social people at all. We'll call them when we're ready to go home, but I doubt they'll come in then, either."

"Well, all right," said Alanna. "Anyway, you kids go and get the horses. Charlie, you can select their rides. Kyle, Sophie, I gather you're expert riders."

"Yes," said Kyle. "Both of us have ridden since we were babies."

"What, like Karate?" asked Josh. "A tradition in the family?"

Kyle didn't respond with the smile Josh expected. "Exactly," he said.

Charlie and Josh looked briefly at each other. Clearly, both of them were becoming puzzled by the twins who didn't seem like anybody else they had ever met before.

"Let's go to the stables," said Charlie and the group walked down the pathway.

At last, Sophie seemed to become normal as they led the horses out into the yard and saddled them. Watching them, Josh decided that the twins really were experts, judging by the easy way they put the saddles on and handled the horses. Sophie really warmed up and began to talk more as she mounted her chestnut mare and gathered the reins.

"What a beautiful horse!" she exclaimed. "This is going to be a wonderful ride."

With all four horses ready, the group moved out of the enclosure and into the wide paddock. The day was beautiful, warm and sunny and all of them, horses and riders seemed to sense the joy of freedom and they set off at a canter.

Charlie and Josh dropped back a little way to observe how the twins rode.

"They're really good," said Charlie. "They both look like they've been riding for years."

"What a weird family they are, though," said Josh. "Karate training from the beginning, horse-riding the same, I bet there's more we don't know yet. And those odd parents who don't want to meet anyone!"

"Not everybody can be as normal as you and me!" said Charlie with a laugh. "C'mon, let's gallop!"

For an hour they raced around the paddocks and ran round the race track that the farm also had and finally began riding back to the stables.

Sophie was laughing with delight and seemed just like any other young girl at last, all anger and coldness gone from her face.

As they approached the stable, something strange happened. Out of nowhere, a huge magpie flew straight at Sophie and cannoned into her face. Sophie screamed and tried to fight the bird, losing her grip on the reins and then fell off her saddle, landing on the ground with a thud.

Charlie was nearest and she jumped off, knelt down by Sophie and held her against her shoulder. Blood was coming from Sophie's cheek and rubbed off onto Charlie's shirt, but she didn't notice.

Sophie was lying still at first, but as her brother joined her, she began to move and mutter something. Josh took out his mobile phone and called Charlie's parents. As he watched Sophie, he saw a small gleam from a pendant hanging round her neck. It looked exactly like the one he had seen hanging from Kyle's neck when they first met for a Karate workout.

"I think she's all right," Charlie said. "The grass is really thick here, looks like she didn't fall hard. But we'd better get those scratches looked at."

"Don't worry about those," said Kyle, helping his sister to her feet. "She'll be fine."

"But she could have a scar!" Charlie protested.

Kyle shook his head. "We heal very quickly," he said. "Don't worry."

At that moment, Alanna arrived in the truck and jumped out.

"Sophie, maybe you can ride back with me, let's have a look at that damage...."

But as she moved to Sophie to examine her face, she stopped.

"Josh, I thought you said she had cuts on her face?"

"But she did!" Josh said in confusion.

But as they all looked at Sophie, they could see nothing at all on her face. There were no cuts, no blood, nothing.

"But there was blood!" Charlie cried. "Look, it's on my shirt!"

"I'm fine," said Sophie. Her bad temper seemed to have returned. "I just want to put the horses away and go home. Kyle, call our parents."

Deciding it wasn't worth arguing, the children led the horses back into the stable and spent the next short period rubbing them down before putting them into their stalls.

As they came out, the big black vehicle was there. The man and the woman got out, looked around then opened the back door for the twins to climb in.

"See you at school on Monday," called Josh.

Kyle waved back but Sophie just looked in front of her and the car drove off.

"Very, very strange," said Alanna. "Anyway, let's get inside and I'll take that shirt for a wash, Charlie."

An hour later, after Josh had joined Charlie and her parents for some scones and tea, he left on his bike. Charlie's father, Greg took the truck to ride round the farm for his usual evening check and Charlie joined her mother in the laundry where there was some washing to do. Charlie always enjoyed sitting with her mother and talking in these periods. She liked hearing about her mother's work as a pathologist, working with the police, though the idea of cutting up dead bodies gave her the creeps a bit.

"Your shirt," said Alanna. "Let's get that cleaned up." She took Charlie's shirt from the pile and looked at the bloodstain for a few moments.

"What's wrong?" asked Charlie, puzzled by her mother's long study.

"This blood," murmured Alanna, more to herself. "It's a bit odd."

"What is?"

"I don't know. Charlie, come up to my office, I want to have a look at this under the microscope."

Intrigued by her mother's behaviour, Charlie followed her mother up to her office where she kept some technical equipment. Alanna spread the bloodstained portion of the shirt under the microscope and studied it for a long time.

"Mother?" said Charlie, worried by what was going on.

"Charlie, I don't want you to say anything to anyone about this," said Alanna.

"But what is it?"

"This isn't like any human blood I've ever seen before," said Alanna. "I'm going to go into my laboratory tomorrow morning and get a better look at it. I can do a DNA check there."

"What, you mean it's not human blood?" said Charlie in horror.

Alanna shook her head. "It's human blood all right, but it's different, I just don't know how yet. I'll know more tomorrow. But remember, not a word to anyone."

"I promise," said Charlie.

But when she went to bed later that evening, she had trouble getting to sleep. Just what was it about Sophie's blood that so worried her mother?

Chapter 4 – The Superhumans

On Monday morning, the three friends met up at the school gates as the big car dropped the twins off. Nothing was said about the accident while riding, but Josh, Charlie and Henry all seemed a little reserved with Sophie and cool towards her.

Kyle stopped Josh before they went to their classes.

"Fancy another workout this afternoon after school?" he said.

Josh laughed. "What and be beaten to a pulp again? You're so far above me, I can't even get you breathing hard! And you're lot better than my Sensei Master."

"Like I said, I've been training since I was a baby," Kyle said with a grin. "But I like being with you guys more than being at home, so we can still get a work out?"

"Well, no problems! I must admit, your parents seem very strange and Sophie is a pain in the neck!"

Both boys obviously were feeling very much at ease with each other and had become close friends in just a few days.

"I like your two friends," said Kyle. "Though it's a bit odd that Henry is so much younger than you and Charlie."

"Oh, that's Charlie!" said Josh. "She's a great one for picking up wounded animals and lonely kids! Henry came here from England a couple of years ago with new foster parents. He's an orphan. Charlie sort of adopted him. But he's a great kid and he somehow became part of the group."

"And what about your family?" asked Kyle.

Josh grimaced. "Not as good as Charlie's. I'm an only child and my parents never seem to know what to do with me. I stay away as much as possible."

"I'm sorry about that," said Kyle. "I really like my parents."

"You never said, where do you live?" asked Josh. "Have you moved permanently up here or are you renting some place?"

"We've got a house up on Franklin Hill," said Kyle. "It's pretty big."

"That's not far from Charlie's place. Maybe we should all visit some day?"

Kyle looked uncomfortable. "Probably not a good idea," he said. "You've seen how antisocial our parents are."

"Well, okay," replied Josh. "I bet Charlie would like you to come riding again at the weekend. At least Sophie seemed more human then!"

"Human!" Kyle seemed startled for a moment, then grinned. "Yes, I suppose you could say that!"

The boys went their separate ways, but Josh decided he had to discuss this latest development of the twins' house with Charlie and Henry.

"Franklin Hill?" Henry looked surprised. "I didn't think there was a property there at all!"

The three had met up during the afternoon break.

"I'm sure of it," added Charlie. "I go riding all round that part and I've never seen a property up there."

"That's weird," said Josh. "He was pretty clear on it, Franklin Hill he said."

"Tell you what," said Henry. "Let's go to the computer room and have a look at Google Earth."

"Great idea!" responded the other two and a few minutes later they were seated round the computer screen as Henry brought up the Google pictures of the local scene.

"That's the road heading up past Charlie's farm," said Josh. "So back a bit... there! That's Franklin Hill."

"And it's as empty as our main paddock," said Charlie. "This is all very curious."

"Why don't we ride up there after school?" said Henry. "Maybe it's just been built after the satellite pictures were taken?"

"Good idea," said Josh. "I've got a workout with Kyle first, maybe after that?"

"Don't tell him what we're planning," said Charlie and Josh nodded.

The three went back to their classes.

An hour later, they met up at the school gates after watching the two boys have another furious Karate session on the lawn. It had gathered a small crowd of other students and they were all highly impressed with the skills displayed.

"He really is incredibly fast," murmured Charlie to Henry.

"Almost super-human," Henry agreed.

Charlie looked at him in surprise. "That's what my mum said."

"What, super-human?" said Henry with a grin.

Realising she'd said too much, Charlie, didn't answer.

They said no more while the two boys did some stretching for a few moments and then joined the other two. Sophie had stayed by the gate, not talking to anyone, seeming to be looking for something in the distance.

At that moment, the twins' car arrived and a man got out, not the two parents.

"Oh-oh!" muttered Kyle. "It's my Uncle Omaron. What's he doing here?"

Sophie however, seemed delighted to see the newcomer, she raced up to him and hugged him.

"You don't like him, Kyle?" asked Charlie.

"I can't stand the man," Kyle replied. "Never could, but he and Sophie have always been close."

The new arrival was standing motionless, staring at the group, his expression not welcoming, not smiling at all.

"I have to go," Kyle said softly. "See you all tomorrow."

Without a backward glance, he walked up to the car, said nothing to his Uncle and climbed in to the back, while Sophie got in the front seat next to the newcomer.

"This gets stranger and stranger," said Charlie. "For a start, that uncle has a really weird name. Let's get out there and see this house of theirs."

A few minutes later, they were riding along the road towards Charlie's farm that was just a couple of kilometres away from Franklin Hill. Another twenty minutes and they turned off the road that led up the hill and stopped.

"There's definitely a house there," said Josh. "But I honestly don't remember ever seeing one before."

"It's a really weird building," said Henry. "It looks more a dome with a couple of spires coming out of the top."

"And I can't see any windows," added Charlie. "Maybe we're just too low to see it properly."

"You know what?" said Henry. "I don't think we should go any further up the hill. There's something freaky about that place and it gives me the chills."

"I think our little mate is right there," said Josh. "This is as near as I want to get to the place."

"I'm with you two," said Charlie. "C'mon, let's go to my place for tea. You know you're always welcome there."

The two boys grinned with delight. They always liked meeting Charlie's parents, and they turned their bikes around and rode back down the hill and along the road to the horse farm.

When tea was finished, Alanna spoke firmly.

"Children, there's something very important I have to say."

She looked so serious that all of them went silent at once.

"I've already discussed this with your father, Charlie and we both agree we need to tell you, but it's absolutely critical that you say nothing to anyone else, is that understood?"

The three children nodded, all feeling apprehensive about what she had to tell them.

"As you know, Sophie spilt some blood on Charlie's shirt on Saturday, though there was no sign of it on her face, not even a scratch when I got there.

But I put that blood stain under the microscope and I could see it was very unusual. So yesterday, I went into my laboratory in town and did some more tests. And I found something almost impossible."

She looked round the table.

"Sophie is human, alright, but she's not like any human I have ever met before. I think it would be more accurate to say that she's super-human. And that means Kyle, her twin, is the same. But the main thing is this. They don't come from our planet Earth."

The three friends stared at her.

"But... where have they come from?" stammered Josh.

"A long way away," replied Charlie's father, Greg. "A REALLY long way away."

"What like Mars, or Venus?" asked Josh and Greg smiled.

"Much further," he said. "There are no other habitable planets in our solar system, so it can't be from there. And the nearest other star to our Sun is Alpha Centauri and that's over four light years away."

"What's a light year?" asked Charlie.

"The distance light travels in a year," Henry answered. "And light travels at over 300,000 kilometres a second, so that's a lot of kilometres."

"And anyway, we already know there are no inhabitable planets there," continued Greg. "So they have to have come a lot further away than that, and I just don't know how they could do that, because nothing is supposed to travel faster than light."

"This is crazy," whispered Charlie. "How can this be?"

Her mother touched her on her shoulder. "It beats me, too, Charlie."

"It's technology so far beyond us, it scares me," said Greg. "But I suppose we've got more to worry about than how they got here. I think we need to think about just WHY they've come."

"Now I think I'm scared, too," said Charlie.

"It's Sophie who worries me," said Henry. "She is really a crabby, bad-tempered thing. Look at the way she reacted to losing at chess."

"But Kyle's great," said Josh. "He and I are good mates."

"Yes, he's lovely," added Charlie and the two boys finally laughed.

"Charlie likes Kyle!" mocked Henry and the parents joined in while Charlie pretended to be angry before she started laughing too.

"But what do we do?" Josh finally asked when the room had gone quiet again.

"Behave normally," said Greg. "That's the safest way. But I agree with Henry, Sophie is the dangerous one. Be very careful with her."

"And then there's the house," said Josh.

"What about the house?" Greg looked interested and Josh explained about seeing the house that had suddenly appeared on Franklin Hill.

"Well, I suppose it could be one of those kit homes you can buy that just needs assembling," said Greg. "They can go up in a few days."

"It's a weird design," said Charlie.

"Tell you what," said Greg. "I'll call the Shire Council tomorrow and ask them."

"That'll be great!" said Josh.

Greg stood up. "Josh, Henry, I'll take the Ute and put your bikes in the back. I'll run you both home."

Gratefully, the two boys agreed. Neither felt like being out alone going past the strange house that shouldn't be on Franklin Hill.

Chapter 5 – The Attack

The next day, Kyle and Josh met up after school again for what had become a regular evening work out at the front of the building. But this time, Josh wasn't quite looking forward to it as he had before. He'd got used to Kyle's extraordinary speed and realised he couldn't match that, but he had already learnt some new moves that delighted him. But after the shocking news from Charlie's mother, he couldn't feel quite at ease with Kyle.

The other boy sensed it.

"What's wrong?" he asked.

Josh tried to hide his worries. "Nothing," he said. "C'mon, let's go. Show me that elbow-strike again."

But Kyle was also a little uncertain. He looked to the school gate where the big four-wheel drive vehicle was parked. They'd both been delayed by school work and it was later than normal. The school grounds were deserted.

"My rotten uncle is here again," Kyle muttered.

Josh looked over at the car. The same man who had picked the twins up before was standing by the car with the door open and Josh could see Sophie sitting in the front seat. The rear door opened and a second man got out. Josh recognised him as the twins' father, but for some reason, he no longer believed in that identity.

Then Josh's nerves began to tighten up. The two men began advancing on the boys and it was clear that they were not in friendly mood.

"Oh-oh," muttered Kyle. "Trouble!"

Josh felt frightened. "Are those blokes as good as you at Karate?" he asked. "Because if they are, I'm no use to you at all."

"They won't be," Kyle replied. "But here, put this round your neck." He pulled the metal strand with the curious gold disc off his neck and handed it to Josh, all the while staring hard at the advancing men.

"What will that do?" said Josh, but he slung the band over his head.

The effect was startling. In just a second, Josh felt incredibly powerful and he sensed that his strength had more than doubled.

"What the...? he said. Astounding elation swept over him, he felt he could have thrown both the attackers to the end of the road and it seemed that the two men were approaching with incredible slowness.

Kyle grinned at him. "Don't talk, fight!" he snapped and then the two men were onto them.

The uncle went for Kyle while the man who had posed as Kyle's father attacked Josh. He was fast, Josh could see that, but whatever had happened to him, Josh now was faster, much faster. His attacker levelled a straight punch at Josh's head, but Josh simply leaned sideways with plenty of time and chopped down at the man's wrist. The man howled with pain and Josh slapped him hard on the side of the head and he went down, quite unconscious.

Kyle was having a harder time of it, but wasn't in any difficulties that Josh could see.

The Uncle went in with feet flying and Kyle easily dodged, spun and kicked the man high on his head. He didn't go down, but said something Josh could not understand and flew at Kyle again. This time, Kyle leaned sideways, the man's driving punch missed his head and Kyle chopped down hard on the Uncle's shoulders and the attacker went down, groaning in pain.

"You're a very naughty uncle," said Kyle with contempt. "I think my parents will not be happy with you."

But Josh wasn't able to see any more. A wave of appalling fatigue washed over him, he felt as if all the strength had drained from his body and he collapsed on the grass as everything went black.

* * *

He had no idea how long he been unconscious when he finally came to. He felt terribly weak and could barely lift his head.

"I'm sorry," he heard Kyle say, as if from a huge distance away, but already his head was clearing and strength was returning to his body. "I had no real idea what the Star would do to you."

Josh was able to sit up and look around. To his surprise, he saw that Charlie and Henry were sitting on the grass too.

"What... what are you two doing here?" he mumbled. He felt a bit sick and swallowed hard.

"We'd both stayed back for music lessons," said Henry. "We just came out as we saw you knock the stuffing out of those two men. You were amazing!"

Josh looked over to the school gates. The black vehicle was still parked where it had been with the doors closed. There was no sign of the two men, nor of Sophie. Kyle was sitting on the grass just a couple of metres away.

"They're in the car," Kyle said with a grin.

"You carried them in there?" Josh said in surprise.

Kyle shook his head. "I got some help," he said and nodded at the school front door. Josh realised that the teacher, Jennifer Hickey was standing motionless, watching the two boys.

"She carried them there?"

Kyle nodded. "She's one strong lady. She's guarding them now."

"She's been watching all of us since you arrived," Josh said. "Why is she so concerned?"

"I think I know," Kyle replied. "I'll check it out soon."

Josh remembered something. Kyle's earlier words were strange.

"What do you mean about what the Star would do to me?"

Kyle took a deep breath. "I knew it would give you some of my speed and power, but I didn't realise how much energy it would drain from you. You Earthlings aren't quite developed enough yet."

Josh shook his head. "You know what, I didn't understand a word of that." He stopped. "Earthlings? Charlie's mother was right then. You're not from Earth?"

"No, we're not. Josh, Charlie, Henry, it's time I told you what was going on. I need to tell you something about my people's history, first...."

Chapter 6 – The Royal House of Yshan

Grand Duke Karocarl, Lord of the Outer Thousand Suns, Grand Champion of the Yshan Dynasty and Commander of the House Guard stared at the man standing before him.

"My brother and his wife are dead?" he whispered in shock. Beside him on the settee, his wife Glendana let out a sob and reached for her husband's hand. The cot containing their new-born twins stood by the settee.

"We are all shattered, sir," said the Fleet Admiral. "As you know, the Emperor and Empress were with us, observing the fleet training manoeuvres by the Cromarn System, something your brother loved to do."

"I know," said the Grand Duke. "There are times when I think my brother would rather be an officer of the fleet than Emperor. Of course, you knew that, you were his instructor at the Fleet Academy twenty years ago and mine three years later."

"He would have been a superb officer," replied the Admiral. "As you have been since. But I simply do not know how this accident happened. Somehow, a missile went off course and struck his cruiser. We lost five hundred officers and crew as well as the Emperor and Empress."

"But Karo, that means…" Glendana couldn't finish and burst into tears.

"Yes, my dear it does," replied Karocarl. "It means I must take over as Emperor until at least the Star can tell us if my brother's little boy is the rightful heir. And the Star will not tell us until the boy is ten, so I must do this for at least eight years. All I wanted was to live a normal life with you and our new son and daughter. It looks like we can't do that yet."

"The Law says we must consult the Star immediately, sir," said the Admiral. "It should confirm you as Regent. The Book says it will glow at least with a partial light if you are the rightful holder of the Crown of Yshan until the boy is old enough to be judged."

"Then let us do it right now," said Karocarl.

Only he, his wife and the Fleet Admiral walked together, out of the living quarters of the Palace and up to the very top of the building to the place that was only visited on very rare occasions when an Emperor died and the Star of the Yshan Kings had to be consulted.

At the top of the stairs there was a massive, black and gold door. It needed no lock for it would only open at the touch of a member of the Royal House.

Karocarl placed his hand on the door which swung smoothly open and they entered the Dome of the Star.

In the centre was a huge black block of pure basalt. The three moved to it and then stopped in such shock that all of them sank to their knees.

The Star of the Yshan Kings had gone.

* * *

It was not the last horrific shock of the day.

As Karocarl returned to his quarters, almost stumbling in his grief and horror at what had happened, a young officer approached them, saluted both the men and handed a note to the Admiral who opened up and drew his breath in sharply.

"Sir," he said, his voice trembling. "It's the Prince. He's gone."

"Gone?" asked Karocarl. "He's surrounded by guards, nursemaids and house staff. How can he be gone?"

"It seems your cousin, Omaron has also gone, sir. It looks like he took him and they have left Home World."

"Could he have taken the Star as well? That seems impossible, the Star can defend itself."

"One of the historians who works on these things has shown that the Star goes into some form of hibernation every two hundred years. It goes almost dead, shows no light, does not react and this period lasts about two weeks. The historian believes such a period is in effect right now and that's why Omaron has been able to remove it and kidnap the Prince as well."

Karocarl stood silently. At last he spoke.

"I have no choice then?"

"No sir," replied the Admiral. "We must have the Coronation at once to confirm you as Emperor Karocarl the Third, Seventy-First Emperor of the Yshan Galactic Empire."

"And here I stay at least until we recover both the Prince and the Star. Admiral, this is not what I wanted."

"I know that, sir. I'll send out search teams immediately. There are only five planets in the entire Galaxy in which a humanoid can hide, so the prince must be hidden on one of those. And we know that the Star sends out a radiation that can be detected within a light year, so we will quite quickly find which planet it is on."

"See to it, Admiral."

"Yes sir," replied the Admiral and for the first time, bowed before Emperor Karocarl the Third, Seventy-First Emperor of the Yshan Galactic Empire.

* * *

"Wait! Wait a minute!" It was Charlie, staring at Kyle with her mouth open in shock. "Are you trying to pull our legs? You're trying to tell us you're from another planet and that there's a Galactic Empire out there?"

"It's more than that, isn't it Kyle?" said Henry. Despite the shock in his face, Henry seemed cool and controlled. "You're telling us that it's your father who is the Emperor, aren't you? This all happened some years ago, right? Those new-born babies, that's you and Sophie?"

Kyle smiled in appreciation of Henry's intelligence.

"Dead right, my friend. Our father is Emperor Karocarl the Third, Seventy-First Emperor of the Yshan Galactic Empire."

"Holy Cow!" said Josh. "I just can't believe all this!"

"I think you should," said a voice behind him. All the children looked up to see that the teacher, Miss Hickey had walked up to the group.

Kyle looked hard at her. "You're not a teacher, are you? Just who are you, Miss Hickey?"

The young woman looked at him and bowed. "Lieutenant Kandria Sestucal, Galactic Fleet, sir."

Kyle looked at the astonished faces of the three kids around him and laughed. "My father sent you to look after me, Lieutenant?"

"No sir," the woman replied. "The Admiral did. I got a face-to-face briefing from him, nobody else knows, not even your father, but the Admiral said he didn't trust the two agents who were sent with you as your parents. I got here some weeks ago."

"Looks like he was right," said Kyle. "Are they both in the pay of my Uncle Omaron?"

"No sir, just the man. He's Captain Marulon Drucsin. The other one is Lieutenant Zenda Hartor and she's loyal. But she's in danger now that your Uncle has appeared."

"And what of my Uncle and this Captain Drucsin? You have them safe?"

The woman nodded. "Both in handcuffs and chained to secure points in the car."

"And my sister?"

"She's your enemy, sir. But I can't handcuff her."

"Kyle, this is all too much!" exclaimed Josh. "What's going on?"

"Let me try and explain," said Kyle. "As you gathered from what I told you before, the Emperor was killed in a spaceship accident. The Admiral doesn't believe it was an accident, he thinks my Uncle arranged it. But my father took over as Emperor, while my cousin, who will be the rightful Emperor when he reaches the age of fifteen in another year, is still a child. But the prince was kidnapped when he was just about two. It looks like my Uncle wants to get Sophie on the Galactic Throne so he can rule through her, but the prince was in the way. And I suppose, so am I now."

"But I still don't get it," said Charlie. "Why are you all here?"

"Because the rightful heirs to the Galactic Throne must prove their claim by holding up the Star," said Kyle. "If the claim is valid, the Star will glow with the light of the entire Galaxy."

"The Star?" said Henry. "You mentioned it before. Just what is it?"

"Maybe I'd better tell you the story," said Kyle. "It starts nearly five thousand years ago when our people had almost wiped themselves out..."

Chapter 7 – 5000 Years Ago
The Rise of the House of Yshan

Garamax Yshan, Leader of the Tribe hunched his shoulders against the cold under the heavy bear skin and plodded wearily back to the village. The hunt had failed, they had found no animals in the forest. His tribe was hungry, beaten by years of warfare with neighbouring tribes and weakened by the damage done to the forests and the migration away by the food animals that had sustained them. There would be no food tonight.

The wise men of the people told him the same story was true around the world. The species was dying out.

"How did we fail so badly?" he had asked the wise men. They had no answers, nor did they know what to do to avert the end of life on the planet.

"Our species will only survive if we had a single leader who could unite the Tribes," said one. "If he could bring such a peace just within our country, that would be a fine start. But then the whole world would have to follow. I have no idea how this could be done."

Garamax Yshan realised he had fallen behind the hunting party on its weary trek back to the village. He had no desire to get back either, no wish to see the hungry, cold faces of the people there, the disappointment as they realised that no new food had been found. His rage and despair suddenly overwhelmed him.

"I call on all the Gods of all the Stars in the Skies!" he roared to the silent trees around him. "Come and explain this! Come and tell me why we all must die! Come and I will fight you to the death for a chance to save my people!"

Nothing but cold silence met his words. Garamax Yshan wept quietly and resumed his walk back to the village.

A few minutes later, as he trudged along a line of bushes, he stopped. A man was standing there. Garamax shrugged the bear skin off his right shoulder and freed his arm with the heavy spear in readiness for combat. It was probably one of the hunters of the neighbouring tribe, also out for one of the almost vanished food animals. This would be a fight to the death, he knew.

"You called us, Garamax Yshan," said the man.

"I called on the Gods," replied Yshan. "You are just a man."

"But I'm not here to fight you," replied the stranger. "So it doesn't really matter what I am."

Yshan realised the man carried no weapon that he could see. He was not even dressed in heavy furs against the biting cold. He wore just thin cloth that fitted close to his body. He had only a small leather bag slung over his shoulder. Yshan had never seen anyone dressed in such a strange fashion.

"Then you must be a madman to be out here without a knife or a spear, no skins against the cold," Yshan replied.

"Not that either. You called for help. That's why I'm here."

Yshan felt ice in his heart. Something was happening beyond his understanding.

"Your wise men are right," said the stranger. "Your world needs a great leader to unite it. We have looked all over the planet and decided you are that leader."

Yshan was struggling to breathe. The man's words should have been nonsense. How can anyone look over the whole world? But somehow, he knew things of vast importance were happening.

"Who are you?" he demanded.

"We are the First," said the man.

"The First?"

"We ruled this world for thousands of years before you came. And many other worlds also."

"This is madness!" shouted Yshan. "How can you rule a whole world? And how can you travel to other worlds?"

"These things you will do one day, also. We left this world and went elsewhere and had no need for worlds to rule any more. Now you can take on those tasks. I will give you the Star."

"The Star?"

The man put down his bag, bent down and opened it. He took out a bundle wrapped in skins and handed it to Yshan.

"Open it," he commanded.

Nervously, Yshan unwrapped the top of the bundle, leaving a layer of skins under it on his hand. He stared at what looked like a massive, white crystal then looked curiously at the stranger.

"Remove the rest of the skins, hold it in your hand and raise it above your head," the man said softly.

Yshan obeyed and almost fainted with shock. The crystal erupted in a massive light, greater than the sun at noon, greater than all the stars in the night sky and lit the forest up like the brightest day. Yet it didn't burn him or blind him. Gathering himself, Yshan stared at the sight.

"That is the Galaxy," said the stranger. "It will only light up like that when the rightful ruler of this world and all the worlds to come holds it. The Star will tell everybody else that the holder rules and all will agree to be led. It may not always be the son of the leader, nor the daughter, but it will tell all who see it that the holder is the rightful leader. Now take it, Yshan, take it around the forests and villages of this country until you have united it and then take it around the world. Your sons and daughters will continue the work until you have a great empire, so long as they rule wisely and with compassion."

Breathing hard, Yshan lowered the Star and wrapped the skins around it. The light dimmed until the Star was just a crystal again.

In front of him, the stranger smiled.

"Now it's time for me to go," he said. In the darkness, he began to glow gently and then brighter until he was almost as bright as the Star had been. His shape melted into a ball of light that rose up to the tops of the trees around them.

"Rule well, Garamax of the House of Yshan," a voice rang out like a musical note through the forest. "And the people will prosper. Always let the Star guide you."

The light vanished and the sound stopped.

* * *

"That was five thousand years ago," said Kyle.

The other three were almost breathless.

"And what happened then?" asked Charlie.

"The first holder of the Star, Garamax, went out the next day and suddenly there were animals again in the forest. He visited the local tribes, held up the Star and all the tribes agreed to unite under his leadership.

Within a year, he had the whole country, within five years the whole world. It's just gone on from there."

There was silence round the group for some moments as each of them struggled to absorb the enormous history they had just heard.

"And what now?" asked Henry. "And again, why is all this happening here?"

"Because when the twins were just weeks old, the Emperor's cousin stole the Star," replied the young woman who they had thought of as their teacher. "We knew that the Star went through a period of hibernation every few hundred years and he obviously watched for it, otherwise it would never have let him carry it away."

"Why, what can it do?" asked Josh.

"It can kill," replied the Lieutenant. "Only members of the House of Yshan can touch it, but it will only glow at its maximum when the rightful heir holds it. One day, perhaps, the Star will decide that another family will rule, but for now, the House of Yshan has kept the agreement and ruled well."

She looked around the group. "And to answer your question, we found that the Star was brought to Earth. We have instruments that can detect the radiation from it and it's here."

"Do you know where exactly?" asked Kyle.

The woman nodded. "Yes, sir, I found it by following your Uncle. But of course, I can't go near it."

"But what of the Prince?" asked Henry. "What happened to him?"

"That's the problem," replied Kyle. "We don't know what my Uncle did. The boy was only a toddler, so probably my uncle killed him. Which means I'm the rightful heir, and I really don't want that. But if I'm killed, then Sophie will become Empress. I know she wants it."

"So what will the Star do if you hold it up?" asked Sophie.

"If the Prince is dead, it will glow like the Galaxy if I or Sophie holds it, and there's no knowing which. If the boy is still alive somewhere, it will only glow a bit for both of us."

The group was silent for a few moments as they all absorbed this astounding information. Then Josh had a thought.

"Kyle, how come I got so strong and fast when I put that medallion round my neck?

"That was the Star," said Kyle. "Every time a new child is born to the House of Yshan, it casts off a tiny fragment of itself. We can wear it and it tends to protect us and give us extra strength."

"And yet I could wear it? Didn't you say it would hurt anyone not of your family?"

Kyle nodded. "It recognises our friends and allies. It decided to help you protect me."

"Wow!" Josh took a deep breath. "It was amazing! But how does it know?"

"We believe the Star is actually a life form," said Kyle. "It knows what's going on around it, it can somehow communicate. But we have absolutely no idea of what it is or where it came from."

"And what of that man who gave it to the first Yshan, what was his name? Garamax?" asked Charlie. "He said something about being *'The First.'* What does that mean?"

It was the young officer who answered. "This is all part of the Yshan legends," she said. "We believe that there was a race of powerful beings who once ruled this Galaxy for thousands of years, but they vanished long before our people developed intelligence. Some of the legends say they will return one day, perhaps to judge how the Yshan Kings ruled. Others believe it will be to wipe us all out if we haven't ruled well."

"Have they ever appeared since then?" asked Henry?

The Lieutenant shook her head. "Never," she said. She turned to Kyle. "Sir, we need to get you all home. I'll take you to the house. Will you three children get home all right on your own?"

Charlie laughed. "If you've got those two men chained up, we should be safe! What will you do with them?"

"There's a secure place at the house," said Miss Hickey. "They'll be safe there and they can't get out."

"But what about Sophie?" asked Henry. "Will you lock her up also?"

"I should," replied Miss Hickey.

"No!" said Kyle firmly. "I'll handle Sophie. She won't be a danger."

"Sir, I really advise against that," replied the young woman. "She's very much allied with the traitors."

"There'll be you and your colleague and me in the house," said Kyle. "That's enough."

The woman said no more but turned and walked to the car.

"We'll see you all tomorrow," said Kyle.

"What, you're coming to school? Both of you?" said Charlie, astonished.

"We need to keep up the game," said Kyle. "Miss Hickey has teaching duties and I'll be safe with her around while her colleague guards those in the house. And I can keep an eye on Sophie while she's with us. After school, we'll go and look for the Star with the Lieutenant."

"Can we come?" asked Charlie.

"Wouldn't do it without you," said Kyle with a grin and Charlie blushed red.

Henry and Josh laughed. "Henry, I'll ride home with you to make sure you're all right," said Josh and the two boys set off together.

"I think something is getting warm between Charlie and Kyle," said Henry as they neared his house.

"Looks like it," agreed Josh. "Hey, do you realise, if that keeps going, our Charlie could become Queen of the Galaxy?"

Henry nearly fell of his bike with laughter. "Do you think she'll let us come and visit her for tea?" he said, chortling.

"Well, why not?' replied Josh, also laughing. "It can't take long for them to get here and back."

"I wonder how they do that?" pondered Henry as they reached his front gate. He unslung his backpack as he opened the front gate and the bag dropped on the ground, spilling some of the contents.

"Darn!" said Henry. "I must have left it unzipped."

Josh leaned his bike against the fence and bent down to help pick up the pens and pencils and other objects lying on the grass.

"What's this, Henry?" he asked, holding up a black cube about the size of a Rubik's game. It was shiny on all side and it seemed quite solid.

"Just something I've had all my life," said Henry. "Apparently I was holding it when I was found abandoned as a toddler. It's all I had and I've kept it all my life, never go anywhere without it."

"It's beautiful," said Josh and handed it over.

"You know I can't invite you in," said Henry with an angry expression as he tucked the black cube away. "My foster-parents don't seem to like my having friends."

"Just like my parents," said Josh. "It's just as well we have a friend like Charlie, isn't it?"

Henry nodded and smiled. "She'd better not go off and marry Kyle then," he laughed.

Josh echoed the laugh, got on his bike and rode home to his equally unwelcoming house.

Chapter 8 - Treason

Josh, Charlie and Henry watched with interest the next morning as the black car arrived at the school gates. Kyle and Sophie climbed out of the back doors but there was no sign of the two people who had posed as their parents.

The three waited by the front door of the school as Kyle and Sophie walked down to meet them. Kyle looked cheerful while Sophie looked really sulky and unhappy.

"So who's driving?" asked Josh.

"The other security guard, Lieutenant Zenda Hartor," replied Kyle. "She's still posing as my mother, but she's generally keeping out of the way."

"And the other two blokes?" asked Henry.

"Securely locked up behind a force field in the house," said Kyle.

"A what?" Charlie was baffled.

"It's like a magnetic field that covers the entire doorway of their prison cell," replied Kyle. "You can't see any sort of door, but nothing can get past it."

They all paused as Miss Hickey walked up to them.

"Good morning, Miss Hickey," said the children in unison, though Sophie stayed silent and looked furiously at the teacher.

"Good morning, children. Everything all right?" she asked directly to Kyle who nodded.

"No fuss at all during the night."

"And Sophie?"

"Don't you dare talk to me!" snapped Sophie. "I'll have you in prison when I'm Queen!"

"Sophie, shut up!" retorted Kyle. He had a great air of command that hadn't been obvious before and it impressed Josh, Charlie and Henry enormously. It seemed to impress Sophie too, because she subsided into a sulky silence.

"Let's meet up after school," said Miss Hickey. "I'll take us to where the Star is hidden."

"Will we be safe?" asked Josh doubtfully.

"As long as you don't touch it," Kyle said. "But we need to see if it will glow fully for us, which means the Prince is dead and I'm the rightful heir, or not. I really hope it doesn't. I don't want to be Emperor."

"We'll meet here at four," said Miss Hickey and they all went to their classes.

* * *

As everybody drifted away from the school after the last classes of the afternoon, the children all gathered by the front gate and waited for the black car to arrive.

All five children climbed into the spacious back of the car to find a space like a lounge room, with three seats in the middle facing backwards. Sophie stayed silent. The driver was the young woman they had thought of as the twins' mother until Miss Hickey had revealed that she was another secret agent protecting the Royal Prince and Princess. Miss Hickey took the seat at the front of the car.

"Where are we going?" asked Josh.

"There's an old building on the edge of town," Miss Hickey replied. "I followed the Uncle there and my instruments revealed some radiation. I couldn't follow him in, but the Star is inside that building, somewhere.

"What happens when we find it, Kyle?" asked Charlie.

"Sophie and I will each hold it up," Kyle said. "It will glow to some extent because we are members of the Royal Family. If the rightful prince, our cousin, is still alive, the Star will know it. But if he's dead, one of us will be the rightful heir and the Star will shine like the whole Galaxy. In fact, it IS the Galaxy, it's actually a three-dimensional map of the entire Galaxy."

"But which one of you will it pick?" asked Henry.

"I've no idea! There have never been twins as possible heirs before. It could decide either of us is the correct one."

"But you said you don't want to be Emperor," said Josh. "Why not?"

"I think it's a horrible idea," said Kyle. "Your life's not your own, you're not free to do what you like, always surrounded by councillors and politicians. I just want to go to the Fleet Academy and become an officer. Maybe I could command a Battleship one day like my father did."

"But you want it, Sophie, don't you?" asked Charlie.

Sophie glared at her and said nothing.

"I just thought of something," Josh said after a few moments of silence. "You've all come from another planet. How come you speak English so well? You can't have developed the same language on a planet nine hundred light years away?"

Kyle laughed. "No way at all," he replied. "But you remember I said we'd been studying you for over a century? Part of the object was to learn the main languages on Earth. We recorded several hundred hours of English, French, German, Russian and several dialects of Chinese and fed the recordings into the computers. Then we'd already developed technology that lets us learn stuff very quickly, by directing it straight into the brain while we sleep. So everybody who comes to Earth can learn a new language in about four hours."

"Four hours?" Josh looked astonished, but he was not alone. They all looked stunned.

"So how many languages do you speak?" asked Charlie.

"Of Earth? Only English," Kyle replied. "We knew the Star was in Australia, so we didn't learn any more than that."

"What about other planets?" asked Charlie. "Do you know any other languages from those?"

"I haven't started that training," Kyle said. "But the only languages we can speak are those of humanoid races and they all seem very similar to humans. There's no way we can even begin to learn the language of non-humanoid species. We have to rely on computer translators for those."

"Could I learn some of your technology that way?" asked Josh.

Kyle nodded. "Easy," he said.

"I think I'd better come to Yshan, sometime," Josh said.

"I'm sure we can arrange that," Kyle said.

Ten minutes later they arrived at a large building that stood in the middle of a vacant plot of land at the end of a dusty stock track that looked like it hadn't been used for a long time.

The Fleet Lieutenant that they knew as Miss Hickey led the way to the front door of the building and they followed her. She held up a small device like a mobile phone and studied it.

"This is odd," she said. "It's still showing some radiation of the Star, but rather less than when I first found this place."

"Can you get us in there?" asked Kyle.

"Of course, sir," replied the Lieutenant and took out another small device, only the size of a memory stick for a PC. She held it against the lock of the door and a few seconds later, a click indicated that the lock was open.

"Let me go first," said the young woman and led the way along a corridor to another closed door. The same approach opened that door and she entered. The rest followed to see a large wooden crate lying in the middle of the floor. The top of the crate was leaning against the wall.

"Oh no!" The young woman let out a cry of despair. "The Star! It's gone."

For a few moments there was silence as deep shock struck all of them. Only Sophie however, did not look distressed. A wide smile of delight spread over her face.

"YES!" she shouted. "We've got it!"

Kyle was shocked and he grabbed his sister by the wrist, so hard that she squealed. Kyle ignored it.

"Sophie! What have you done?"

She wrenched her arm away.

"You think I'll let you become Emperor?" she shouted. "You're too soft to rule the Galaxy. You don't even want the crown, how can you be a ruler if you don't want the job?"

Kyle's face was white. "It's not our choice," he said. "You know that as well as anyone. The Star tells us who will be Emperor."

"I don't care about the Star," she said. "If nobody can see it, nobody can tell. I'm the Princess and I've as much right to the throne as you do. At least I want the job, so I'll do it better than you could."

"And what about the Prince?" asked Kyle. "He's the rightful heir if he's still alive."

"He's been gone for twelve years," said Sophie. "Our Uncle took him away and dumped him somewhere. He's almost certainly dead."

The Lieutenant had recovered her self control.

"Sir," she said. "We should go back to the house and talk to your Uncle. We may be able to convince him to tell us where the Star is and what he did with the Prince."

Kyle nodded. "Let's go. Keep an eye on my sister."

The group walked out of the building and got back in the car. Nobody spoke all the way back to the house on Franklin Hill.

* * *

"This place still gives me the creeps," Henry said as the car drove up the hill and stopped by the strange structure. Now that they were parked beside it, they could see that it looked like it was made of metal.

"Like an upturned pudding bowl," said Charlie. "No windows, anywhere? Kyle, what sort of house have you built here?"

"I'll explain later," said Kyle. "Let's get inside."

Cautiously, Josh, Henry and Charlie climbed out and followed the twins and the two woman officers inside. The front door slid aside like an elevator door to reveal a huge open space. A circle of lounge chairs sat in the middle with coffee tables before them, but there seemed little else to make a comfortable home. No pictures hung on walls, no bookshelves, no obvious television or stereo system could be seen.

Charlie saw a circular rail against one side and decided it must be a staircase to a basement and sure enough, Miss Hickey walked to that and descended. The others followed, except for the woman who had been driving. Charlie hadn't heard her say a word so far. She was quite similar to Miss Hickey, tall and slim, short hair and she looked very athletic. She stayed upstairs while the rest descended.

Downstairs was even bleaker than the upstairs. No seats of any kind were in the middle, and there were just doorways around the space, but there were no doors. In two of them, there were rooms behind the doorways, well lit up and standing there were the two men who had attacked Kyle and Josh.

Kyle took command. "Lieutenant, put my sister in a cell."

Sophie screamed with fury and struggled, but she couldn't fight free of the grip Miss Hickey had on her shoulder and she was pushed gently but firmly into the room next to the Uncle. Miss Hickey pressed a switch and nothing seemed to happen, but Sophie tried to walk out of the room and was blocked by something invisible, as if she had walked into perfectly clear glass.

Kyle turned his attention to the other man. "Who are you?" he said firmly.

The man looked frightened. "Captain Marulon Drucsin, Galactic Fleet, sir," he replied.

Kyle shook his head. "Not any more, you're not. You'll face trial for treason when we get home, but I don't like your chances."

He turned to the other cell. "So, Uncle Omaron, you were trying to break the Law of the Star?"

The man sneered at him. "The House of Yshan has become soft," he said with contempt. "We needed stronger hands. The Emperor was weak, your father is no better, nor are you. Your sister has the strength the Empire needs."

"What have you done with the Prince?" asked Kyle. "You kidnapped him when he was just two years old. He'll be fourteen now, almost old enough to be Emperor."

"I brought him here, to Earth," replied Omaron. "I kept him in Stasis on my ship for a few years then dropped him in the middle of some country as far away from this region as I could, then I brought the Star here. After that, I don't know anything."

"What, you just abandoned him?" asked Henry. "What happened to him?"

Omaron shrugged carelessly. "I've no idea. Maybe he died, maybe somebody adopted him, I don't know."

"The poor little boy," said Charlie. "What a rotten thing to do."

Omaron glared at her for a second then looked away.

"Where's the Star, Omaron?" asked Kyle.

"Well hidden," replied the man. "You might be able to detect the radiation, but you can't pinpoint its exact location within fifty kilometres."

"Omaron!" shouted Kyle in frustration. "What's the point of all this? The Star has served us for five thousand years! The Empire runs smoothly. Why are you trying to ruin all this?"

"The Empire needs new blood and a new hand on the wheel. The current line of the House of Yshan is weak and stale. Your sister has the strength that you don't."

Omaron turned away and sat down, ignoring Kyle and looking at the floor.

"Sir, let's leave them," said the Lieutenant and Kyle nodded, moving to the staircase and followed by everybody else.

Upstairs again, Kyle looked helplessly at the two Fleet officers. "So what can we do?" he asked.

"We must keep searching," said Miss Hickey. "Perhaps I should call the Admiral to send more troops?"

Kyle shook his head. "Not yet. I don't want the countryside crawling with strange people, it could cause all sorts of problems."

"I know what we do right now," spoke up Charlie.

The others looked at her.

"It's getting late," continued Charlie. "I think we should all go back to my house for dinner, and Kyle, you must stay there tonight. I hate the idea of you sleeping in this creepy place with those creepy people downstairs. I bet my mum and dad will know what to do."

"An excellent idea," said Miss Hickey. "I'll drive you."

Gratefully, the others agreed.

* * *

Miss Hickey declined the invitation for dinner.

"No Ma'am," she said to Alanna. "I'll join my colleague and keep guard over the prisoners."

"The what?" exclaimed Alanna, startled.

"We'll explain, Mother," said Charlie.

"I certainly hope so," said Greg. "All right, Miss Hickey, but thank you for bringing the children home."

"She's Lieutenant Kandria Sestucal, Galactic Fleet, dad," said Charlie with a wide grin.

Her parents stared at her.

"I think we'd all better sit down," said Alanna.

It took Kyle nearly half an hour to explain the whole story to Charlie's parents. They weren't as astounded as they might have been and Charlie decided that was because they'd already discovered that Kyle and Sophie were something more than human.

"It's an Empire that rules over the whole Galaxy?" Greg asked in fascination.

"All of it," agreed Kyle. "But that only means about fifty intelligent species and we have no communication at all with some of those, so we just ignore each other. The rest are really part of a federation and the Empire just keeps the peace. We don't rule in any real sense and there's no need for taxes and that sort of stuff, because with such a huge number of worlds, we can take anything we need from uninhabitable worlds without damaging anything. So we're all very rich, really!"

"And how far away is your home planet?" asked Alanna.

"Quite close, really. Only about nine hundred light years."

"Only nine hundred...." Greg took a deep breath. "And how long does it take your ships to travel that distance?"

"Just over two hours," said Kyle.

"TWO HOURS?" Greg looked like he'd been hit by a sledge hammer.

Alanna laughed. "Before Greg took over this farm from his father, he was professor of astrophysics at Sydney University. This sort of stuff interests him!"

"We need to talk more, young man," said Greg. "Or should we be calling you Your Royal Highness?"

"Please don't," begged Kyle. "I hate all that nonsense. As I've told the others, I don't want to be Emperor. My dad was a space fleet officer before he had to leave and become Emperor when my uncle died and that's what I want to do. Honestly, when we find the Star, I'm dreading holding it up and the whole Galaxy shines out. That would mean the real prince is dead and that's a horrible idea. I never knew him, but I want to meet him."

"So he'll be about fourteen now?" asked Alanna and Kyle nodded.

"Another year and he can become Emperor if we find him. If we don't, my father stays in the position and then presumably me, unless the Star says Sophie will be Empress."

"Okay, let's get back to the problem of finding the Star," said Greg. "You said we can't actually pinpoint the radiation?"

"No, we can't."

Josh finally joined in. "What about that thing round your neck? Didn't you say that was actually part of the Star?"

Kyle reached into his shirt and drew out the medallion, laying it on the table.

"Good heavens!" exclaimed Greg as they all stared at it.

It was about the size of a fifty-cent piece, but looked like pure gold. In the centre was a brilliant white spark. There were no markings anywhere to be seen.

"Kyle, is that dangerous?" demanded Greg with alarm.

"No sir, just very bright. Actually, that's the brightest I've ever seen it."

Alanna slung a tea towel over the disc. "It's hurting my eyes," she said. "So does Sophie have the same thing?"

"She does," said Kyle. "I wonder why it's suddenly got so bright? And I wonder if Sophie's has done the same?"

"Hmmm..." said Greg and got up from the table, walking out of the room. The others looked puzzled, but a few minutes later, he returned carrying a helmet with black eye shields.

"My welding hat," said Greg and put it on, pulling the tea towel off the medallion and putting it to his face. A few minutes later, he covered the medallion again, took off his helmet and placed it on the floor.

"That's amazing," he said. "I can't actually detect anything there. It's too small to see with the naked eye. I'd like to get a microscope onto it."

"It would have to be a very powerful microscope," said Kyle. "That particle is only a few molecules off the main Star."

"And does it somehow communicate with the Star?"

"It's believed so. We haven't actually found anything that we can detect, though."

"Interesting...." murmured Greg. "Can you leave it with me?"

"For a day or two," Kyle said.

"Okay, time for dinner," said Alanna. "Josh, Henry, call home. You're all staying here tonight."

"Yay!" said Henry.

"What he said," added Josh.

"And me," said Charlie and blushed.

Chapter 9 – The Search for the Star

The next two days passed quietly. The kids went to school and the Fleet officer guarding the prisoners wrote a note from Sophie's "mother" that she was unwell and would stay home.

As school ended, Charlie got a call on her mobile phone.

"Mum and dad want us to go round there for tea. Okay with you two?'

Wide smiles from the boys indicated that everything was indeed okay with them and they went to collect their bikes from the shed.

Half an hour later, they were sitting at the table in the dining room and Greg joined them. He grinned cheerfully and placed an object about the size of a book on the table. The others stared curiously at it. Finally, Josh pointed at it and spoke.

"That's Kyle's medallion in the middle, but it's almost covered with wires and things. And that looks like a car satellite navigation system. What on earth is it?"

"It's what we call a breadboard design," replied

Greg. "This is what the technologist builds first so he has room to attach bits and pieces but once everything has been tested, it can all be miniaturised. I reckon I could have that down to the size of a mobile phone if I worked on it, but we only need one."

"And what is it, dad?" asked Charlie, looking proudly at her father. "You've gone back to being an electronics genius, have you?"

"I call it the Star Trekker," said Greg with a laugh. "Actually, it's a homing device for the Star."

"Wow!" shouted Kyle in excitement. "You mean you can find the Star with that?"

"Indeed I can," replied Greg. "I found that the tiny fragment on your medallion was emitting some sort of pulse. But it was also receiving one. It was obvious that it was talking to its parent, the Star. I managed to link it into the satellite navigation device so that it tells us where to head, though I've no idea how far away it is."

"That's incredible!" said Kyle. "We never did that at home, but I suppose we never needed to. Nobody has ever stolen the Star before."

"Probably right," agreed Greg. "No point in inventing something that has no use!"

"When can we set off and look?" asked Kyle.

"Not till the morning," said Alanna. "Then Kyle, you can call your two guardians and we can all go in that enormous truck of yours. Boys, you're all staying here again tonight, so call your parents. And now it's dinnertime!"

* * *

Miss Hickey arrived at eight in the morning with the massive car and everybody piled in, though with four children and two adults in the back compartment, it was fairly crowded. Only after everybody was in, did they realise Sophie was sitting in the front seat.

"Why is my sister here?" asked Kyle. His tones were chilly.

"If we find the Star, you know both of you have to hold it," replied the officer. "I have handcuffs on the Princess, there's nothing she can do."

Kyle nodded with just one freezing look at Sophie then ignored her for the rest of the trip.

Miss Hickey started the car and drove away from the house.

"Head South!" called Greg as the vehicle pulled onto the main road and when they reached the highway, the direction remained the same.

"This could be a long trek," commented Alanna. "I hope your Lieutenant is okay driving all day, Kyle?"

Kyle grinned. "If she graduated from Fleet Academy, she's done a lot worse than spend the day driving! And remember, while she's not of the royal family, she's still Yshan! We have considerably more strength than Earthlings."

"I'm still having trouble getting my head round all this," said Alanna. "Suddenly, we have to cope with the fact that there's a Galactic Empire out there, with some fifty superior species and travel around the Galaxy is common and fast!"

"Most people can't cope at all when they first hear about it," said Kyle. "That's why we're so very careful before we introduce ourselves to a new race. Earth was scheduled for an introduction in about fifteen years."

"You mean you've been studying us?" Charlie asked. "How long?"

"About a century," said Kyle. "It should have happened already, but this world has been a bit unstable for a while now. It may have to wait even longer before things settle down."

"Well, I hope they hurry up," said Charlie. "It sounds like a pretty good Empire to me and then I could travel all over the Galaxy!"

"Maybe we can arrange that anyway," said Kyle.

"She takes second place after me," said Greg decisively. "I'm the astrophysicist here, remember! If anyone's going travelling round the Galaxy, it's me!"

The conversation was becoming quite excited when suddenly Greg called out to the driver.

"Hang a right!"

The car slowed and turned onto a ramp off the highway, on to a bridge over the highway and began travelling west.

"And left!" called Greg after just a couple of kilometres. "Down that road! I think we're getting close!"

More slowly now, they navigated along a country road and then turned off onto a rough track that led up to a large but very battered shed in the middle of a grassy paddock.

"Here, Greg?" said Alanna doubtfully. "It looks a most unlikely place."

"Here," said Greg firmly. "In this building."

Silently, the group climbed out and stood by the shed. Miss Hickey joined them and took out her detector.

"Yes," she said. "This is the sort of radiation level I found before in the other place. The Star's here, all right."

"Let's go," said Kyle with authority and walked in. The rest followed and found an empty space, with sunlight coming in from gaps in the roof and the walls.

"Pretty decrepit," muttered Josh. "It doesn't look like the safest place to store something."

Greg was walking around, stamping on the floor at spots.

"There's a space underneath," he said. "Hey, look, some old rakes against the wall. Grab them and start raking the straw off the floor."

The boys each took a rake and began clearing the floor. After only ten minutes, Henry called out.

"Here! There's a trapdoor!"

"Stand back!" called the Lieutenant. "It may be booby-trapped."

While the rest stayed by the wall, she examined the door with her small electronic device.

"Not booby-trapped," she said after a few minutes. "But there's a force field over it. Nothing serious. It was obviously intended to keep ordinary people out, not somebody with our technology."

A moment later, she stood up. "That should do it," she said.

A few seconds later, the trapdoor was open and Miss Hickey was peering into the space. The little device hummed briefly and then shone a bright beam into the darkness.

"There's a ladder," she said. "I'll go down first."

She descended down the ladder and then called to the group who all cautiously climbed down into what was now a well-lit space. As with the last time, there was a wooden crate in the middle of the basement.

"My turn, I think," said Kyle and advanced on the crate. The lid was not nailed down and he slid it aside. He stared down into the crate.

"Sir?" asked the Lieutenant.

"It's here," said Kyle. "But I really don't want to hold it up."

"Sir, you must," said the Lieutenant. Kyle nodded and bent down, lifting up an object wrapped in black cloth. He held it motionless for a moment then carefully removed the cloth until he held it in two hands.

It looked like a huge crystal, about the size of a football. Beyond its size, it didn't look out of the ordinary.

"You must hold it up," urged the officer. "Above your head, please sir, this is critical."

"I know," said Kyle and lifted the crystal in both hands until his arms were straight.

The crystal suddenly blossomed with light that made the one the officer had used look quite dim. Kyle lowered it and the light faded again.

Charlie realised that she hadn't breathed since Kyle had brought the Star out of its case. Now she let out her breath with a gasp and Kyle smiled at her.

"The light was strong, but it wasn't the light of the Galaxy. I'm not the rightful heir. Either it's Sophie or the real prince is still alive. Sophie, your turn."

He waited while Sophie walked slowly to him as she stared at the Star. The Lieutenant removed her handcuffs. Kyle handed the crystal to his sister.

Sophie took a few deep breaths then suddenly raised the Star above her head.

Kyle let out a gasp. The Star had not changed at all. Sophie brought it back down and stared at the object, her face white.

"Sophie, let me see your medallion," said Kyle, the authority in his voice so strong that Sophie didn't hesitate. She reached into her shirt and pulled the medallion out. The disc was the same gold as Kyle's was, but there was one huge difference.

The fragment of the Star in the centre of the medallion showed no light all.

The area was dead silent. Somehow, the Earthlings all understood.

The Star had rejected Sophie completely.

Kyle stood straight and tall, his face calm and relaxed.

"The Royal Prince, the rightful heir to the Throne of the Galactic Empire is still alive," he said.

And then Henry moved. He walked deliberately up to Kyle and placed his hands on the Star.

"Henry, what are you doing?" shouted Kyle in great shock. "This thing will kill you!"

Henry didn't reply. He took the Star from Kyle and raised it above his head.

And the light of the entire Galaxy blazed in the basement of an old shed in the middle of the country.

Chapter 10 – The Future Emperor of the Galaxy

The scene stayed frozen in time for several moments before Henry lowered the Star and stood staring at it, his face expressionless. Charlie and her parents and Josh all looked stunned, unable to move and could do nothing but stare at the scene. Charlie realised that Kyle, Sophie and the Lieutenant they had known as Miss Hickey had all sunk onto one knee, bowing to Henry.

"Please stand up," said Henry, his voice shaky. Kyle was the first to do so and he moved to Henry, took the Star from him and wrapped it up again before placing it back in the wooden crate.

"How did you know?" Kyle asked.

"I didn't," replied Henry. "I had no idea. I just was overwhelmed! I knew I had to take it from you. It can't be real, can it, Kyle?"

"I'm afraid it is, Henry. You are Garamax the Nineteenth, Seventy-Second Emperor of the Yshan Galactic Empire. Or you will be when you turn fifteen next year."

Henry's face looked like he was feeling ill.

"Who's Garamax?"

"You are, Henry. That was your father's name and he gave it to you. It was the name of our first great king and it has a long and honourable history."

"I don't like it," said Henry.

"I promise you, I'll always call you Henry," said Kyle.

"But what do you mean, I turn fifteen next year?" said Henry. "I'm nine."

Kyle shook his head. "No, Henry, you're fourteen and you're older than Sophie and me. When Uncle Omaron kidnapped you, he kept you in stasis for several years while he hid from our fleets. That means he kept you frozen in a special device that stopped all your body developments including your mind, so you stayed exactly like you were when you were two years old. He only released you from that when he brought you to Earth and left you in the streets to be found."

Finally, the others recovered from the shock of the last few minutes. The Lieutenant approached.

"We need to get you all back home and safe, sir," she said.

Kyle laughed out softly. "Is that 'sir' to Henry or to me?"

The officer smiled. "Both, sir. But we really must head back."

"Okay," Kyle said with a nod. He looked down at Sophie who was now huddled up on the floor and weeping. "You too, Sophie," he said firmly. He reached down and took her arm to help her get to her feet, but she shook his hand off.

"Don't touch me," she shouted.

Kyle looked in despair at Charlie's parents. Alanna seemed to understand and approached Sophie quietly.

"Come on, Sophie, we need to get you home and into bed. You're quite ill," she said gently.

Sophie seemed to respond to the touch and let herself be lifted to her feet and led out to the car where Alanna placed her in the front seat as the others followed into the back.

"She should be all right now," said Alanna. "But Lieutenant, I think it would be safest for all of us if you restrain her."

"Agreed, Ma'am," said the officer and snapped a strap round Sophie and locked it into place before moving round to the driver's seat and setting off in the direction of home.

"Shall we lock the Princess in the cells when we get back, sir?" The Lieutenant seemed to be addressing both Henry and Kyle together. Henry looked frightened.

"Kyle, is she talking to me?"

Kyle laughed. "I don't think the Lieutenant is quite sure, herself! We're all a bit gobsmacked by what's happened."

"Then would you please stay in charge?" said Henry. "I just can't cope with all this."

"I think that would be best for now, if you approve. Lieutenant, is that all right with you?"

From the front seat, the young officer replied. "I believe that's the best course of action until the Crown Prince gets used to the idea."

"The what?" whispered Henry.

"The Crown Prince," said Kyle. "That's you, Henry. And you realise, don't you, that Sophie and I are your cousins?"

Henry seemed to be looking into the distance and didn't reply.

"Lieutenant," said Kyle. "When we get back, I don't see any need to restrain the Princess in the cells. She seems quite severely in shock and I doubt she'll be a problem again."

"I agree, sir," replied the Lieutenant.

"So do I," said Charlie's mother. "And I'm the doctor here. I think she's in what we call a catatonic state. Kyle, you seem to be handling this amazingly well. Considering what's happened, how are you staying so calm?"

Kyle looked thoughtful. "You know, Mrs Foster, I was asking myself that, too. I think I'm just so relieved that I don't have to face being Emperor one day and can concentrate on getting to the Fleet Academy and becoming an officer like I've always dreamed."

Charlie moved closer to Henry and put her arms round him.

"You're shattered, aren't you, Henry?"

He rested his head on her shoulder almost like a toddler. "I just don't understand any of this," he whispered. "I knew I had to take the Star, but everything that's happened since, this is all impossible. I know I'm just nine year old Henry Jackson and somehow I also seem to be the Crown Prince of a Galactic Empire, and I'm really fourteen and in another year I'll become Emperor. It's insane!"

"It'll all settle down soon, I promise you," said Kyle.

Henry looked up at him. "We're cousins?"

"We surely are!" replied Kyle. "My father who is right now standing in as Emperor, is your uncle. His brother, who was the Emperor until he was killed, was your father."

Henry stirred and sat up straight. "There's something...." he muttered softly and reached inside his jacket pocket.

Josh recognised what Henry pulled out.

"It's that black cube!" he said. "I didn't know you had it with you!"

"I always have it with me," replied Henry, staring in fascination at the object. Then he touched his fingers to the side and without a sound, the cube opened up. Inside was a gold disc, exactly like the ones that hung round the necks of Sophie and Kyle.

In the middle of the disc, the tiny fragment of the Star of the Yshan Kings glowed like a tiny sun.

"Now I know who I am," said Henry.

* * *

The rest of the ride home passed in silence as everybody became absorbed in their own thoughts, trying to absorb and make sense of the events of the day.

Only the Lieutenant spoke as she called up her colleague on her own communication device and reported the events and developments.

As they drove up to the strange house on Franklin Hill, Alanna broke the silence.

"Kyle, I think all of you should stay at our place tonight. Let Miss Hickey take Sophie to the house and she and her colleague can guard her and the two captives, but I think Henry needs our company tonight."

"Good idea," said Kyle, but the Lieutenant had other ideas.

"No, Ma'am," she said. "I can't leave the Crown Prince on his own without Fleet protection."

"He's got all of us around him," said Greg. "What harm can come to him?"

"Probably none," replied the officer. "But as a Fleet Officer, I'm now duty bound to guard my Crown Prince and future Emperor."

"Good grief!" murmured Greg. "So will you stay in our house tonight as well?"

"No sir," she said. "I'll patrol the area during the night."

"Don't you ever get any sleep?" said Charlie in distress. "You've been on duty all day and driving all this time. When do you get some rest?"

"She's Yshan," broke in Kyle. "We can manage with a lot less sleep than Earthlings and we're a lot stronger, too. And then she's a trained Fleet Officer. You'd be amazed by what she can do!"

"No, I don't think I would," said Greg with a chuckle. "I think I've had an overdose of amazement from you people, already!"

The Lieutenant got out of the car as her colleague approached from the house.

"Everything all right, Zenda?" she asked the new arrival.

"Calm as a summer's day," she replied, the first words any of them had heard her speak. "The prisoners have been silent since you left."

"Good," the Lieutenant said as the others climbed out of the car. As Henry got out, the second officer snapped him a sharp salute. Henry looked startled.

Miss Hickey gestured at her colleague. "I think we'll pass on all the ceremonies, Zenda," she said. "The young man is a bit shattered by all this and he'd prefer we treat him just as before."

"I understand," said Zenda. "But can I just say, sir, how delighted we all are that we've found you?"

Henry looked back calmly and smiled. "Thank you," he said.

"He's starting to take control," Kyle murmured to

Charlie and received a bright smile in return.

"Sophie, you come with me," said the officer and led off her off with a strong hand on Sophie's shoulder.

"She's not treating her like a princess," commented Charlie.

"Nor can she," replied Kyle. "The Star has withdrawn her royal status and now she's just somebody who has tried to break the law of the Empire."

"But doesn't that distress…" began Charlie and stopped as she saw tears rolling down Kyle's face.

"She's still my sister and I love her," he said.

Greg put a friendly hand on his shoulder. "Let's go home," he said. "I think we need a quiet evening with friends and without any earth-shaking events."

"That would be wonderful," said Kyle, wiping his eyes and everybody climbed back in the car for the short drive to the farm.

And that's how the evening was, quiet, friendly and relaxed while Lieutenant Kandria Sestucal of the Imperial Galactic Fleet, somebody they had once known as Miss Jennifer Hickey, a teacher at the school, patrolled the area around the house.

All seemed peaceful in the morning. After a major breakfast of bacon, eggs and toast, Charlie announced her decision to saddle up a horse and go riding while Kyle said he needed to go back to the house. He wanted to try and talk to Sophie but said he also had to communicate with the home planet, talk to his father and report on everything that had happened.

"Talk to home?" asked Greg with interest. "It's nine hundred light years away! How do you do that?"

"There are ways of transmitting instantaneously across any distance," Kyle replied. "Something to do with quantum mechanics, I believe."

Greg looked thoughtful. "Ah!" he said. "I need to go and think about that!"

"Well, don't ask me about it!" said Kyle. "But when you come to Yshan, I'll find you a couple of people who can tell you all about it."

Greg took a deep breath. "I'll hold you to that," he said.

"Time to go, gentlemen," said the Lieutenant. "We need to check in with my colleague."

The three boys followed her out to the car and a few minutes later arrived back at the strange metallic house. All of them jumped out together and went up to the front door which was hanging open.

"That's not good, sir," said the Lieutenant. She carefully pushed open the door and slowly walked in. The house was deadly silent and there was no sign of life in the room. The young officer put her fingers to her lips for silence and moved to the staircase.

"Oh no," she whispered and moved swiftly to the ground where the body of Lieutenant Zenda Hartor lay sprawled on the carpet. She placed her fingers against the other woman's neck and concentrated. Finally, she let out a sigh of relief.

"She's alive, but she's in deep shock," she said. "She's been hit by a stun gun. Josh, can you call Charlie's house, get her mother out here? She needs a doctor."

Josh pulled out his mobile phone as the Lieutenant stood up and surveyed the room. The two cells were dark and obviously empty. She moved to one wall and pushed a button. A panel slid back to reveal nothing but metal racks, all empty.

"They've got the stun-guns," she said. "All three of them. This is bad. I can only imagine that Sophie released the prisoners."

"Are you armed?" asked Kyle.

"There's a gun in the car, sir," she replied. "I'll try and get it and hope they're not watching."

"If you go out alone, you're a single target," said Kyle. "We need to do a rush for the car. One of us should get through and get the gun."

"I'm in," said Josh, despite a wave of fear through his body.

"Me too," said Henry.

Both the elder boys turned on him. "No, Henry, you have to wait here, you're too young."

Henry let out a loud laugh. "Hey, I'm older than you two, remember! And I'm the Crown Prince. You think I'd let people take risks I can't take?"

Kyle looked seriously at him. "You're growing up, cousin. All right, we run out of the door, spread out, race as fast as you can, zig zag a bit, get to the car."

"The gun's under the driver's seat," said the Lieutenant. "There's a red spot on the handle. Press that and the safety's off. It's got a conventional trigger like any pistol. Point and shoot, it'll knock out anyone in its path."

Josh found he was breathing deeply, struggling to control his nerves but he forced himself to move with the others to the front door.

In silence, they positioned themselves. The Lieutenant first pointed at Josh, then in the direction he should run. She repeated the process with the other two, then held her hand up and silently counted down from five with each finger folding as the time proceeded. As her last finger went down, they all shot out of the door and raced in their allocated direction.

Almost immediately, the air crackled round the young woman and she let out a sharp cry and folded to the ground.

"Keep going!" shouted Kyle but it was too late. Kyle's uncle, the second man and Sophie all appeared by the car, weapons in their hands pointed at the three boys.

They stopped

Sophie walked up to Henry, a wide grin on her face.

"Do you seriously think I'd let some silly little boy take my throne from me?"

Henry just stared calmly directly into her eyes. It seemed to disconcert her and she dropped her gaze, turning to her brother.

"You're a fool, Sophie," said Kyle. "The Star has abandoned you, how can you ever hope to become Empress?"

"Easy!" she snapped. "With you and that little boy both removed, I'm the only choice, I'm the only member of the Yshan royal family. The Star will have to name me!"

Kyle shook his head. "That's not how it works, Sophie, you should know that. The Star has stayed with the House of Yshan because we have always managed to have a worthwhile heir. You know it's not always been the son of the Emperor, sometimes it's been the daughter, sometimes neither and another relative has been found suitable. But they've always been good, honest people, not rotten to the core like you and our uncle. If you're the last of the House of Yshan, the Star will probably decide a new House will take the throne after five thousand years. And you know what? I think that will be a good idea."

Sophie looked furious, so angry that her normally pretty face was twisted and ugly.

"You're wrong, brother. With you two out of the way, I'm the only choice and I'll have the crown."

"Don't be a fool, Sophie," replied Kyle. "You have to stand in the public square and hold the Star up. It won't glow for you and the Golden Mask won't fit you. It means the Imperial Fleet will not support you and the people won't either."

Josh had been listening to all this, but he was also hearing another sound in the trees around them. With an explosion of bushes, a horse burst from the forest and galloped straight at the group by the car. Charlie was in the saddle. She drove the big stallion at the two men holding the guns. They had no time to turn before the horse broke them both down and rode over them. The horse stopped and reared up in front of Sophie who screamed and tried to bring her gun up, but a hoof hit her shoulder and she went down, the gun flying into the distance.

Kyle moved with the lightning speed that he had shown in Karate. He leaped at the unconscious men on the ground, gathered up their weapons then raced over to pick up Sophie's gun also.

Charlie calmed her horse and grinned at the boys.

"Good morning, gentlemen," she said. "Nothing like a girl on a horse to save the day, is there?"

An hour later, the two Fleet Officers had recovered under the care of Charlie's mother, but both were still rather shaky and weak. The two men were back in their cells, as was Sophie who sat silent and sullen as

Kyle pushed her gently into the space and hit the switch that set up the force field.

"The two men need hospital," said Alanna. "They both have broken arms and very bad bruising. Sophie's badly bruised, too."

Kyle shook his head. "That would be a terrible mistake. Can you imagine what will happen as soon as a doctor examines them and sees the bloodstains like you did? We just can't let the world know about the Empire yet, it will cause chaos."

"But you can't just leave them in pain like that!" protested Alanna.

"Not a problem Ma'am," said Miss Hickey. She still looked groggy and her face was pale, but she was a lot better than before when she could hardly walk. "We have repair kits here, those arms and bruises will be healed by tonight."

"Oh my!" said Alanna. "I wish I could have some equipment like that!"

"That would be the same as having local doctors examine them," said the officer with a smile. "We can't let this be known until the world is ready."

"But we all know about the Empire," said Greg, walking up. "How are you going to stop us telling the world?"

The Lieutenant let out a shaky laugh. "I couldn't stop you at all," she said. "But do you think anyone will believe you? They'll just laugh and think you're crazy!"

"Hah!" said Greg. "Yes, I suppose you're right. So what happens now?"

"Now we go home," said Kyle. "We have to take the Star and Henry home and confirm his position as heir. And next year when he turns fifteen, he'll become Emperor. My father will be seriously happy, so will everybody."

"But this is a major problem," said Alanna. "It means Henry will vanish. How is that going to look? What will his foster-parents say? How about the school? The police will start investigating a possible murder or abduction and you know what? Greg and I, Josh and Charlie, we'll be the major suspects. This could get very difficult for us. We could all end up in prison."

"No chance," said Kyle. "We have a way of handling that. We've got a device that can be set very accurately to block all memories of events or people. We'll make sure that nobody on the planet has any memories at all of Henry at all and if they come across a document with his name on, somehow they just won't see it."

"Everybody on the planet?" broke in Charlie. "Does that mean us? Do you mean we won't be able to remember Henry either? That's horrible!"

Kyle grinned widely. "Yes, everybody on the planet at the time we release the blocking process. That's something I want to talk to you all about."

"But you said you'll be going home," said Alanna. "Does that mean you'll have a spaceship of some sort coming for you?"

"No need," replied Kyle, still grinning cheerfully.

"No need?" echoed Alanna. "Why not? How will you get home?"

"The ship's already here," said Kyle.

"What, in orbit or something?" Josh had entered the discussion and was looking enthralled.

"No," said Kyle. "It's been here all the time. This is it. You're standing in it."

After all the shocks they had sustained in recent days, this was perhaps the biggest for Charlie's family and Josh. Only Henry seemed undisturbed and that made Charlie and Josh look at him carefully. He'd been completely silent since they returned to the house, saying nothing as Sophie and the two men were placed in their cells.

"Henry!" exclaimed Charlie. "Something's changed about you! What is it?"

Alanna moved to him and carefully looked at his face. Then she stood back and studied him intently.

"Henry, you've grown at least five centimetres since this morning. And you look older. How do you feel?"

"Strange. Confused." Henry looked at her and tried to smile.

"Your voice has changed," said Charlie. "It's deeper, more like Josh's."

"I think Henry's catching up on the years he had in stasis," said Kyle. "He's becoming a real fourteen years old. The Star must be doing it."

"That seems to be it," said Alanna. "I can see why this is uncomfortable for you, Henry. I can only assume it will settle down soon."

"This is a spaceship?" Charlie's father broke out of his astonished silence. "It can fly nine hundred light years in a couple of hours?"

"Much further than that," said Kyle. "We can cross the entire length of the Galaxy in the same time."

"That's a hundred thousand light years!" said Greg. "In two hours?"

"There's no difference, once you enter the worm hole," replied Kyle.

"This stands all of physics on its head," muttered Greg. "But the theory's been talked about for years. I wish I could see it!"

Kyle looked across to the two Fleet Officers and seemed to have a rapid, unspoken discussion before nodding at them. He turned back to the others.

"We'll be leaving at any time. Can I suggest something?"

"What's that?" asked Greg.

"Go home, get a couple of days of clothes and anything else you may need, like a toothbrush. Josh, I think anything I have will fit you."

He looked round the group and smiled.

"I think you should all come to Yshan and see Henry's confirmation as the next Emperor before the people of the Empire."

Chapter 11 – Travel to Yshan

"Just take your seats," said Lieutenant Kandria Sestucal of the Imperial Galactic Fleet.

"Anywhere?" asked Josh. "These are just armchairs. Don't we have to strap in or anything?"

"No need," replied the officer. "It's all very smooth. Actually, we took off as soon as you came in."

"What?" Greg exclaimed. "But we felt nothing! No acceleration, nothing?"

"Nothing, sir," replied the Lieutenant. "Let me show you something."

She did nothing that anyone could see, didn't press a button, didn't wave a hand, but a large, rectangular area about five metres long and two metres high appeared on the wall. For a second or two it appeared to be jet black then something appeared.

"It's the moon!" shouted Josh. "Holy Moly, it's the moon!"

The arc of the moon's surface spread across the entire viewing port.

"We're just five thousand kilometres above its surface," said the Lieutenant. "We didn't need to come this close, but it's a chance to give you a view very few people have ever had."

"Good heavens!" said Greg rather more softly. "That took less than five minutes! What sort of engines do you have?"

"Gravity engines," she replied. "So they act on every atom of the ship, including the people in it. That's why you feel no acceleration, you didn't need straps on take-off and you didn't even need to sit down!"

"But the gravity on the floor seems normal," said Greg. "You have that much control?"

"We do," she replied. "Once we discovered that ability, everything became a lot easier."

"Can I see the engines?"

"Of course, sir," she said and waved to her colleague. "But you'll be disappointed! There's just a couple of grey metal boxes about the size of a tea-chest down in the basement. And I can't open them up! Zenda," she said as the other officer walked up. "Take our guest and show him the engines."

Alanna chuckled as her husband was led away. "Once an astro-physicist, always an astro-physicist, I suppose!" she said. "Charlie, your dad's in his own personal heaven!"

"Wait until he sees us enter the worm-hole," said Kyle. "That will just blow his mind!"

"When does that happen?" asked Josh.

"Just under an hour," Kyle said. "Now that we've

gone past the moon to give you the scenic tour, we can't go out past the other planets, much as I'd like to show you them. We have to stay quite slow while we're in the solar system, that's all the planets going round the Sun, because if we start flying at near the speed of light, we'd cause major problems for all your astronomers."

"Why's that?" asked Charlie.

"It's our gravity engines," said Kyle. "They exert so much power, they'd actually distort space! And that would make the view through the telescopes go strange, too. Any astronomers watching that area of space would get a nasty shock. All that would cause too much disruption and we mustn't do that."

"So what do we do?" asked Josh.

"We head out at ninety degrees from all those planets' orbits, straight out and then we can accelerate until nearly the speed of light until we can head for the wormhole."

"And then what?" asked Alanna.

"Impossible to describe. Why don't we wait until then? Meanwhile, I think Henry's feeling a bit lost."

They turned to see Henry sitting alone in one of the seats in the middle of the area.

"Oh rats!" said Charlie. "We've all been so gobsmacked by this, we've forgotten about Henry. Josh, let's go and talk to him."

Henry stood up as Charlie and Josh reached his seat.

"Holy Moly!" said Josh. "Henry, you're taller than I am! You were just a little squirt yesterday!"

"Weird, isn't it?" said Henry. His voice was as deep as Josh's now, almost a man's voice and his face had got slimmer with lines of maturity that had not been there the day before.

"How are you feeling now?" asked Charlie. "Any better?"

"Just fine," he said. "While I've been sitting here, I think the Star has been teaching me stuff. I think I know about Yshan history now and a little about some of the other people around the Galaxy. But I still can't really get it that I'm going to be Emperor."

"We're going to miss you horribly," said Charlie, tears in her eyes.

"Hey," said Henry and put his arms round her. "You won't have to. If it's only about two hours space-flight, you can come and visit often enough. Heck, you can come for a long weekend!"

"But how are we going to get there?" Charlie's voice was muffled.

"Easy!" said Henry. "I'll be the Emperor, right? I bet I'll have a personal space-ship to take me all over the Galaxy. I just come and get you any time!"

"Wow!" said Josh. "I never thought of that! Just think, Charlie, we can travel around the Galaxy in our personal luxury space-ship!"

Charlie laughed and Henry let her go. The three friends sat in the armchairs and for the next half hour talked about the happy times as kids they had shared since they all met up.

* * *

"Wormhole coming up," said Kyle from across the room. "This you need to see."

Josh, Charlie and Henry went over to join him and Charlie's parents who were all standing by the viewing port.

"How were the engines, Dad?" asked Charlie.

"Like Kyle said, just two grey metal boxes," said Greg with a laugh. "Very dull and quite boring if I hadn't known what they were!"

"How far are we from Earth, now, Miss Hickey?" said Josh then looked annoyed. "Sorry, I still think of you as our teacher!" he said.

"Not a problem, Josh," she replied. "I enjoyed my time as a teacher! But anyway, we've been travelling for fifty minutes at quite a bit below the speed of light, so we're about seven hundred and fifty million kilometres away."

Greg was silent a moment. "We're travelling about a million kilometres every four seconds? A bit over eighty percent the speed of light?"

"That's about right," she said.

"I can't help being a teacher," he said. "And I never expected to see this sight in my life. Children, look at the stars ahead. What do you see?"

Josh and Charlie looked for a moment. "They're blue!" said Charlie.

"Why's that, Mr Foster?" asked Josh.

"It's called Doppler Shift," said Greg. "We see it in telescopes, but nowhere near as strong as this. If a star is getting closer, the light shifts to blue and if the star is receding, it shifts to red. But we're moving so fast towards all those stars, the blue shift is immensely strong. It's quite amazing!"

The Lieutenant broke in. "And in just a few seconds...."

They all turned to the blackness of space outside.

"The stars have turned white again," murmured Charlie.

"We've stopped," said the Lieutenant. "Now watch."

Outside looked quite featureless. But in a shocking explosion of light, a fiery red ball burst into view. In just seconds, the massive inferno expanded in a vast circle of red, yellow and blue flame that filled the entire view ahead. Inside the circle was pure black. Everybody except for the fleet officers and Kyle drew back in shock.

"A worm hole," said Kyle.

Greg swallowed. "We've had theories about this, but nobody has ever worked out how it could happen. Where does that thing lead?"

"Almost everywhere in the Galaxy," replied the Lieutenant. "We discovered how to open up a hole a few centuries ago, but it took a long time to work out how to navigate through them and a lot of ships got lost millions of light years away and never returned.It's possible some even crossed into other galaxies, but we have no way of knowing."

"And how do you do it now?" asked Greg.

"VERY carefully," replied the officer with a smile. "It's all matter of entering the wormhole at exactly the right angle and exactly the right speed. That's what the computers are calculating now. It will take about a minute."

In utter fascination, they all waited. Then a tiny movement of the immense ring caught Josh's eye and he realised the ship was moving. There was no sense of acceleration nor any indication of the direction, but with an almost frightening surge, the huge ring of multi-coloured fire seemed to rush at them and they hurtled past the wall of flame. Then there was absolute blackness.

Josh realised he was holding his breath and let it out in a long, slow gasp.

"What now?" he heard Greg ask.

"Just a few more seconds," the officer replied and as she finished speaking, the reverse action occurred. With a soundless flash, the ship flung itself out of the ring of fire which vanished and in front was an ocean of brilliant white stars.

"We're here?" Greg asked.

"Not quite," the Lieutenant said. "But we're over nine hundred light years away from where we were!"

"Good grief," muttered Greg. "They'd never believe this back at the University!"

"No point in trying to tell them, either!" replied the officer. "But you'll be the only person on Earth who knows it works!"

"How long to Yshan now?" asked Josh, still feeling breathless at the sight he had just seen.

"About an hour," she said. "But I think... ah yes! Look out there!"

Charlie stuck her face by the viewing port.

"I can't see anything.... OH!"

What had seemed at first just some meteorites moving suddenly expanded at an astounding rate and in front of them appeared a spaceship. It was not at all like the vessel in which they were travelling. This was massive, it dwarfed their ship so that Josh felt like he was standing on a rowing boat before an ocean-going cruise liner.

Even more astounding was the huge number of other ships all arrayed in neat lines ahead of them. But the lines went back into the distance.

"Six hundred and forty ships," said Kyle with immense pride. "The entire Imperial Fleet has come from every sector of the galaxy."

He turned to Henry. "And they're all here to say hello to you, Henry."

Henry didn't reply. He was standing motionless by the viewing plate, head held high. His face displayed huge pride.

Charlie looked at Josh and smiled.

"Now he looks like a prince," she murmured and Josh could only agree. Henry looked every inch the Crown Prince of the Royal House of Yshan, the emperors of a galactic empire for five thousand years.

"The Fleet Admiral is coming over," said Kyle. "He's taking a shuttle over and it will dock with us."

"What, no beaming over like in 'Star Trek'?" asked Josh, only half in jest.

"It's never worked," said Kyle. "Great idea, but nobody could ever develop it. We can transmit objects, but they're a horrible mess when they arrive. Hard to imagine what a human body would look like, but nobody's willing to try."

"Ugh!" said Charlie.

They all heard a small bump somewhere under the ship.

"The shuttle," said Kyle. A moment later, a solitary man appeared up the stairs from the basement.

"Follow the rituals, Henry," murmured Kyle closer to Henry's ear. "This is all tradition and you'd better get used to it!" Aloud, he spoke again.

"Your Royal Highness, may I present to you, Fleet Admiral Dromas, Commander of the Eight Sectors of Your Imperial Fleet and your loyal servant."

The Admiral was a tall man with a craggy, distinguished face that reflected a habit of being in command. His uniform was dark blue with the only badge of rank that Josh could see was a coat of arms in gold on each sleeve cuff. His cap looked like any military officer's on Earth but had no gold braid or other decoration except for the same coat of arms on the front. The Admiral stood straight and snapped a smart salute at Henry.

"Your obedient servant, Sir!" he said. "And may I welcome you back safely to Yshan? We are all grateful that you have returned."

Henry smiled, seemingly quite relaxed and proffered his hand for the Admiral to shake. "Thank you, Admiral. I think we all owe our thanks to these wonderful people here."

The tall man looked at each in turn and smiled. "Indeed, the Empire is grateful to all of you. Please let me know if there is anything we can do to repay you."

"I know what Greg wants," said Kyle. "Admiral, he wants to talk to some of our engineers about wormholes, exceeding the speed of light, gravity engines and quantum communications!"

The Admiral grinned cheerfully at Greg. "I think we can keep you very busy for the next couple of days, sir! But of course, you'll be there to see the confirmation of Prince Garamax as the rightful heir to the throne."

"Drat, I *really* hate that name," muttered Henry, but only Josh and Charlie heard him.

"Don't worry, you'll always be Henry to us," whispered Charlie.

"Okay, then that's all right," said Henry. He turned to the Admiral.

"Admiral, I think you'd better take us home."

The officer saluted again and left to return to his monster ship.

Chapter 12 - The Presentation of Garamax the Nineteenth, Seventy-Second Emperor of the Yshan Galactic Empire

"I still can't believe what I'm seeing," Charlie's father muttered, staring down at the world of Yshan. "I'm in orbit around an inhabited planet, nine hundred light years from Earth!"

The others seemed just as shaken as they peered out of the viewing screen.

"It never loses the thrill for me," said Kyle, standing with them. "That's why I'm so happy that I can go ahead and join the Fleet Academy and see lots and lots of worlds all over the Galaxy."

"I wish I could do the same thing," said Josh. "That would be so cool! It would be a lot better than living at home!"

"Kyle, can you tell us what's down there?" asked Charlie. "Where's home?"

"We're coming round to it," said Kyle. "Look, we've got three main land masses, all of them spreading from almost the North Pole to almost the South Pole. Then there's the Girdle, that's what we call the chain of islands, thousands of them spreading all round the equator and over a thousand kilometres wide."

They all studied the strange geography of the new world that seemed so different from Earth. As they travelled round, a new land mass came into view.

"That's Callatrom," said Kyle. "The whole land mass is one country and the Imperial City is up there, about half way up to the pole, by the coast. We're heading there right now."

As they watched, the ground grew closer until they saw mountains and rivers, then roads and several cities, one of which began to grow larger and larger in the viewing screen.

"It looks like Canberra!" said Alanna with a laugh. "All circles and a lake in the middle!"

"It's very beautiful," said Kyle. "We'll be down in a minute. We'll just leave quietly, there's a car waiting for us, no massive reception or anything, 'cos I think Henry's had enough shocks today!"

"Good idea," said Henry with a smile. But he seemed quite calm and composed.

"I still can't believe how you've grown and changed in just a few hours," said Charlie. "Is the Star doing that?"

"I think so," said Henry. "What do you think, Kyle?"

"Probably," agreed Kyle. "But this has never happened before, so nobody really knows. Have you been getting Yshan history?"

"That and a lot more," Henry replied. "I know what your father looks like, I know what's going to happen at the ceremony tomorrow and I've learned a lot about the politics. It seems that being Emperor is not just ceremonial, like the Queen in England."

"No, it's really not," agreed Kyle. "You're also president of the governing body, whichever political party is in power. You have real power. That's why it's so critical that the Emperor is a good person, too. But the Star always seems to ensure that."

"That's scary," said Henry. "But I'm glad. I didn't want to spend all my time at ceremonial occasions, opening bridges and museums and stuff."

"You won't!" said Kyle. "It's a real job. And we're here. Let's go and meet my father and mother and then we can have a quiet evening together, all of us."

"What about Sophie?" asked Josh.

"My father will be talking to Sophie," replied Kyle. "And I don't think she's going to enjoy the experience."

And with that, they left the space ship for their first breath of the air of an alien planet.

To Josh's relief, there was no guard of honour, no ceremony, just a salute from a uniformed driver of a vehicle a little bigger than the machine they'd driven in back on Earth, then they were silent as they studied the streets of the Imperial City of Yshan until they reached the palace.

Henry decided that he really liked his new Uncle and Aunt and they got on wonderfully. The conversation over dinner was happy and cheerful.

"We're both so happy you've come back," said Glendana, the twins' mother. "It's not just that we can step down from the throne next year, Karo never wanted the job at all, but it's wonderful that you're safe again. We've all been so frightened, not knowing if you were alive or dead."

"It's certainly been a different life that I had," said Henry. "But maybe it helped me in my new job. Now I know what life is like for the ordinary person."

"I think that's right," said Karocarl. "Still lots of training for you during the next year, though."

"I'll be there to help him," said Kyle.

"What's going to happen to your Uncle and that other bloke?" asked Josh.

Karocarl frowned. "They'll both be tried for treason as well as kidnapping in the case of my cousin, Omaron. They'll be exiled to another planet to live as ordinary people and never be allowed back to Yshan. The Fleet Officer will also be court-martialled and dishonourably discharged, probably some prison time as well."

"And what about Sophie?" asked Henry. "How will she cope with all this and what will you do with her?"

"I'm glad you mentioned that," said Karocarl. He nodded at a waiter standing by the door and he walked out. A moment later, he reappeared, saying nothing, but behind him, looking terrified was Sophie. She stood motionless by the door until her father waved her closer.

She walked up and stood just a metre from Henry.

"I'm so sorry," she whispered. "I think I just got too crazy at the idea of being Empress."

Henry studied her. "And so now what, Sophie? What do you want to do?"

"I want to be part of my family again," she said. "I want to be Kyle's brother, your cousin and I know that the Star has said I can't be in line for the throne any more. But I promise I'll be a loyal subject of the Emperor."

"Can we be sure of that?" asked Henry.

"I know so," said Kyle. "Look at her medallion."

Around Sophie's neck, her gold medallion began to glow like it had before it went out in the shed on Earth.

"The Star has accepted her," said Karocarl. "She's a member of the royal family, again. But Sophie, you don't get away with this completely."

Sophie said nothing but she looked anxious.

"You go to the planet Heridam," said Karocarl. "You'll spend five years working there helping old people in retirement homes. It's not a rich, glamorous place, you'll live like one of the people and you'll get your education at the Yshan Embassy school. You do not have the rank of Princess during that time and nobody will know who you are. When you're sixteen, you can come home again."

"Yes, father," Sophie whispered.

Henry grinned and took Sophie's hand.

"Why don't you pull up a seat and join us for dinner?" he said.

* * *

The morning was bright, mild and perfect. Henry had been dressed in a pure white suit, almost like a navy officer's tropical uniform, but the only decoration was the Imperial coat of arms on his chest. It was the same badge as the Fleet Admiral had worn on his cap.

"I'm nervous," said Henry.

"I've no doubt," said Kyle with a friendly smile. He wore a similar uniform and badge, while Sophie wore a beautiful white dress. "It's not every day somebody gets presented to three hundred billion people around the galaxy as their future Emperor!"

"We'll be with you every step of the way," said Charlie. "Can I give the future Emperor of the Galaxy a hug?"

"Oh please do!" said Henry and smiled happily as Charlie put her arms round his neck for a moment.

"What happens now?" asked Josh.

"Now Henry rides in an open carriage from the palace to the stage in the middle of the city. He sits with my father and mother and we'll follow in the next carriage."

"Wow!" said Charlie. "It's like being in the royal wedding procession!"

Four officers of the Imperial Fleet appeared at the door and gave a smart salute to Henry who drew himself up and returned it like any senior officer.

"Let's go," he said and they escorted him from the room.

"We'll go out by another doorway," said Kyle. "Our carriage is waiting there."

Ten minutes later, Josh, Charlie and her parents, Kyle and Sophie found themselves following a carriage with Henry and the twins' parents riding out of the palace gates. Dense crowds lined the streets.

"I thought they'd be cheering," said Alanna. "Is something wrong? Everybody's so silent."

"But listen carefully," said Kyle. "It's a happy silence. Look at the faces, they're smiling. We Yshans are not a cheering people, it's not part of the culture."

Charlie and Josh looked around and Kyle was right, everybody did seem incredibly happy.

"It's okay if you wave at them," said Kyle, turning to the crowd and waving. "Everybody knows the part we've played in returning the Crown Prince to his home."

For the next few minutes, the group in the carriage waved around the crowd. Henry's carriage was just about fifty metres ahead and when it arrived at a large stage, it stopped while the second carriage diverted round behind the stage where it stopped also.

"We get out here," said Kyle, "and we take seats at the back of the stage before Henry and our parents enter."

They followed that instruction and sat down at the back, staring out at the massive crowds in front of them.

"This is weird," said Charlie. "There must be a million people out there. All looking at us!"

Then Henry and the Emperor and Empress appeared and the low murmur of the crowd disappeared as everybody went quite silent. Josh watched them take throne-like chairs at the front of the stage and realised that there was a black block standing at one side, with a velvet cloth over the top.

"The Star is there," murmured Kyle, seeing Josh's look. "There's also the Golden Mask in another case next to it."

"What's the Golden Mask?" Charlie spoke softly in the dense silence of the million watchers.

"You'll see," whispered Kyle. "Now watch."
Emperor Karocarl stood up and went to the black block. He slipped away the velvet cover and revealed the huge white crystal that was the Star of the Yshan Kings.

A sigh of awe ran through the crowd.

"This is the only time the people see the Star," whispered Kyle. "This is the object that has ruled

our history for five thousand years. It's the biggest moment in our lives."

The Emperor picked up the Star in two hands, turned and faced Henry who stood up. The Emperor moved to Henry who turned to face him and Karocarl carefully handed the Star to him.

Henry turned to face the front of the stage and with a decisive motion, raised the Star above his head in both hands.

Even in the light of a bright day, the Star erupted with brilliance. The huge spiral of the Galaxy glowed like a thousand suns, throwing shadows round the city and drowning almost everything in light.

This time, the crowd's sigh of awe was ten times louder, it was also a sound of huge happiness and delight. They knew that the next Emperor was with them and they had the protection of the Star.

Henry held the Star like that for over a minute before lowering it and the light of the Galaxy dimmed. He carried it back to the black stand and replaced the cover over it.

"Now the Golden Mask," whispered Kyle. Tears were running down his cheek and Josh saw that the same was happening with Sophie. But their faces were not sad, rather filled with pride and joy.

Emperor Karocarl went back to the stand, bent down behind it and brought out a circular tray of what looked like black basalt. On it was a golden mask. To

Josh, it looked like the mask of an ancient Egyptian Pharaoh, perfect in its pure lines.

"The final sign," murmured Kyle. "The rightful heir must put on the mask and it will take on the features if he's the right one."

Henry held up the mask for all to see, then carefully slipped it against his face.

Almost immediately, the metal seemed to flow like mercury, taking on the shape of Henry's face until it looked just like a golden replica of their friend.

Again, the crowd sighed with mingled awe and delight.

The new Emperor had been confirmed.

* * *

"I don't want to go," said Josh. Tears were in his eyes, but he was not alone. All of them were struggling to keep their composure.

"I don't want you to go, either," said Henry. "But you know you have to. But I'll send the ship for you in the next school holidays, so you can come and visit."

"Try and stop usP a g e | **134**," said Alanna. "I want to see more of this lovely planet."

"Here's an idea," said Kyle. "Josh, when you reach fifteen, come back and apply to the Fleet Academy with me."

"What? You mean I really could?"

"You'll need a lot of catching up in our technology," Kyle said. "But our teaching machines will help you and if you worked really hard every time you get here, I think we can swing it. But you're a citizen of the Galactic Empire, even if Earth doesn't know it yet, so you can apply."

"Wow!" said Josh in excitement.

"And I want to study some of that too," said Greg. "I know I can't pass it on to anybody, but I really, really want to learn about some these things and perhaps visit a few more planets."

"Easily done," said Kyle."

"And what about Henry's absence?" asked Alanna.

"All taken care of," said Kyle. "Nobody will remember him and nobody will be able to see any papers with his name on them. It's not a hundred percent perfect, so occasionally, somebody may see the name but it won't mean anything. As far as Earth is concerned, Henry was never there."

It took a while for them all to part. There were hugs and handshakes and quite a few tears, and only the knowledge that they'd all return to Yshan in a few weeks allowed them to make their final goodbyes and enter the spaceship.

Two hours later, they were back on Earth.

Chapter 13 – Epilogue

The School Speech day was going well. Most of the prizes for academic subjects had been presented and speeches made and Josh had covered himself with glory for his first ever prize in a school subject for his short story about travelling through space to another world. The English teacher had praised it for its extraordinary imagination in its description of travelling through a wormhole across a thousand light years.

Charlie had won a prize for mathematics and both she and Josh were sitting on the stage with the other prize winners when the next prize was announced.

"And the trophy for the school chess championship goes to Kyle Ellem," said the Principal and applause rang though the hall as a young Grade Five boy walked up.

"That would have been Henry's again," murmured Charlie to Josh who grinned at the thought.

The Principal lifted the small silver cup and looked with a puzzled expression at the base where the names of previous winners were engraved.

"Henry Jackson?" he said. "Who on Earth is Henry Jackson?"

Josh and Charlie looked at each other.

"Well, he's not on Earth, that's a fact," murmured Josh and he and Charlie burst out laughing.

Part Two

The War of the Yshan Empire

Chapter 14

The wedding of Kyle Yshan, Duke of the Moidari Sector, Guardian of the Six Home Planets and newly commissioned Sub-Lieutenant in the Yshan Galactic Fleet to Charlotte Foster, only daughter of Gregory and Alanna Foster of New South Wales, Australia, Planet Earth was truly a grand affair.

The ceremony took place in the Royal Palace on the Home World of Yshan and was attended by dignitaries from over a hundred planets within the Yshan Empire as well as the graduating year from the Galactic Fleet Academy, two hundred young men and women who had all become officers just two weeks before. They were all in their "Ceremonial Whites," beautifully cut white tunics with the tiny gold star on their shoulders to signify their rank, black belts and officer-pattern swords with gold handles and their names engraved on the blades.

Also in attendance was His Imperial Majesty, Garamax the Nineteenth, Seventy-Second Emperor of the Yshan Galactic Empire. He sat in the front row with Charlotte's parents, dressed simply in a smart suit so as not to distract attention from the bridal couple. Sitting in the same row were Kyle's parents, previously the Emperor and Empress of the Yshan Empire, who had occupied the throne as

Regents while the search for the last Emperor's kidnapped son had been in progP a g e | **142**ress.

Standing next to the groom as Best Man was Joshua Bradshaw, born on Planet Earth and like the Groom and the two hundred young people in white, a newly commissioned Sub-Lieutenant in the Yshan Imperial Galactic Fleet.

When the ceremony had been completed by Fleet Admiral Dumar Domas, Commander of the Eight Sectors of the Galactic Fleet, the Best Man drew his sword and joined the young officers to form two lines holding their swords up, tips touching in the middle as a grand archway for the newly married couple to walk down.

The bride looked quite stunning and her parents both had tears running down their cheeks as she walked past them with a beautiful smile in their direction. Josh could hardly believe this was the little tomboy who had been his friend at school and he felt his heart turn over with pride as he looked at her and the groom, Kyle, his best friend since they had met when both were eleven years old.

As all royal weddings must, the ceremony was completed by a carriage ride through the city before returning to the Palace. Crowds lined the streets and shouted with delight. The newlyweds rode in the first carriage, the Bride's parents rode in the second with the Emperor and the groom's parents who had been Emperor and Empress themselves until the new Emperor had been proclaimed the rightful occupant of the throne by the Star of the Yshan Kings. As a young boy, he had held up the Star and it had glowed with the light of the entire Galaxy, saying firmly that this was the rightful Emperor.

Eventually, the royal procession returned to the Palace

and the small group that would be at the reception left the carriages and entered the dining room. But before the dinner began, the main characters joined the Emperor in his private quarters.

All bowed deeply and the two young men threw their best salutes at their Commander in Chief.

The Emperor sighed. "Don't come the raw prawn, you guys! This is Henry, remember?"

Laughter broke out freely among the group. When they had all met, Henry had been a scrawny little boy, apparently two years younger than the others and a lot smaller. The tall, handsome young man in his mid-twenties bore little resemblance to long-ago Henry.

"That's better," Henry said with a wide grin. "Have you any idea how boring it is always to have people bowing and scraping before me? Let's forget all that royalty stuff for now, eh?"

He walked up to the bride and hugged her firmly. "Charlie, you are absolutely gorgeous! Congratulations! And to you too, Kyle! You couldn't have chosen better!"

"Don't I know it, Henry!" replied Kyle. "I think I always knew it when we met as kids back on Earth."

"On another subject," said Henry. "How's Sophie?"

A frown appeared on Kyle's face. "I don't know," he replied. "She's vanished. You know your Uncle, my father sent her into exile on the planet Heridam for five years. When she was able to leave, she didn't come back to Yshan saying she was going travelling, but she's disappeared."

"Hmmm..." Henry looked uncertain. "You know, Kyle, I really don't trust her. I know she was accepted again by the Star and she said she wanted to be a loyal member of the Yshan family, but there's just something about her."

"I know," said Kyle with a nod. "Still, there's not much she can do on her own."

"Agreed," said Henry with a huge smile. "Anyway, far more important things to think about! You and Josh are joining the Fleet next week?"

"Yes, we are!" chimed in Josh standing nearby. "We're both assigned to the battle cruiser "Garamax Fourteen.""

"So not a long honeymoon for Kyle and Charlie," said Henry.

"That's the life of a Fleet Officer's wife!" said Charlie with a laugh. "We both know it and it's just part of what we've agreed to."

And with that, the group broke up to join the formal celebrations in the dining room.

Chapter 15

"Good grief, it's ginormous!" said Josh.

"Always an impressive sight, an Imperial Battle Cruiser," agreed Kyle.

The two young men looked through the pilot's screen as the shuttle slowly approached the massive warship hanging in orbit round the Home World of Yshan. The shuttle travelled along the entire length of the half-kilometre long cruiser which seemed almost to dwarf the planet below them.

"Who's the captain, do you know?" asked Josh.

Kyle shook his head. "I don't. I heard that Captain Ashorn has been promoted to Commodore and taken a place at Fleet Headquarters, but I don't know who replaced him."

"Well, we'll find out in a few minutes," said Josh. "We're docking."

An enormous, circular door opened in the side of the cruiser, looking like a camera lens. The shuttle slowly passed through the entrance and with a gentle bump, touched down on deck. A small door opened in the wall. Carrying their bags, Kyle and Josh climbed and found themselves in a large hangar with a number of smaller shuttles lined up in several rows.

The War of the Yshan Empire

An elderly man with the stripes of a senior non-commissioned officer snapped a smart salute at the arrivals. A little self-consciously, Josh returned it, noting that Kyle seemed quite accustomed to being saluted.

"Chief Petty Officer Karlon, sirs!" he said. "Please leave your bags here and somebody will take them to your quarters. Captain asks that you report immediately."

Kyle and Josh exchanged curious glances. This was unusual. But they followed the elderly CPO as he led through a series of corridors and up two flights of stairs before reaching a door to a cabin. The CPO tapped on the door, opened it without hearing any instructions and saluted smartly to somebody in the room.

"Sub-Lieutenants Yshan and Bradshaw reporting, Captain," he said and stepped backward out of the room. "In you go, gentlemen," he muttered and Josh was sure there was a small smile on the man's face.

He and Kyle stepped inside the cabin, repeated the CPO's salute and stood to attention. But Josh let his astonishment take over.

"Ms Hickey!" he gasped, then flushed with embarrassment.

The tall woman standing by a desk smiled.

"That's *Captain* Kandria Sestucal, Lieutenant Bradshaw," she said. "Welcome aboard, both of you. At ease."

Stifling their astonishment, Josh and Kyle removed their caps and relaxed. It had been twelve years since they had met what they thought was a new teacher at the school in Australia, only later to learn that she was an officer in the Galactic Fleet, sent by the Fleet Admiral to act as guardian to Kyle and his sister Sophie on their mission to Earth to seek out the Star of the Yshan Kings.

"Our congratulations, Captain," said Kyle, seemingly far more in command of his emotions than Josh.

"Thank you, Mr Yshan," the Captain replied. "Let's sit down."

She took a seat at a coffee table and the other two took her lead and sat down.

"You've come a long way for a young Earth boy, Mr Bradshaw," the Captain said. "I was delighted that you were able to get into the Fleet Academy. You're the first Earthling ever to do it."

"I had good connections, Ma'am," said Josh. He was still feeling stunned and also delighted at the discovery of the new Captain's identity.

She shook her head. "Connections don't do it," she replied. "Not even Duke Yshan, nephew of one Emperor and son of the last Emperor could have made it without passing a severe battery of tests, just as you had to. You earned your place."

"Thank you, Ma'am," said Josh, feeling a huge glow of pride.

"Now I understand that you displayed an extraordinary capacity for galactic navigation," the Captain continued.

"He was top of the class all the time," chimed in Kyle.

"So I see. I have your records here, of course. I read the thesis you did for your graduation. *"Wormhole Strategy in Fleet Attack."* I was most impressed. So I'm assigning you to the Navigator's section. And Lieutenant Yshan, I need you in the Gunnery Section. That was your strength at the Academy, I know. We have a new breed of torpedo on board and you must become totally familiar with them very quickly. There's somebody here who can help with that."

She touched a button on the table. "Ask the Technical Director to come in, please."

"Technical Director, Ma'am?" asked Kyle. Josh knew that this was not a standard role on board a warship.

The Captain smiled as the door opened to reveal a quite unexpected person.

"Greg!" said Kyle in delight as Charlie's father walked in. "I didn't know you were here. And WHY are you here?"

Greg laughed and hugged his new son-in-law. "I designed these new torpedoes," he replied. "I've been supervising their loading and set-up."

The Captain stood up. "Okay, gentlemen, report to your stations. We're about to get under way. We're patrolling the Zambartri Sector for the next two weeks and we'll be testing these new torpedoes during War Games."

Josh and Kyle rose to their feet and replaced their uniform caps. They snapped immaculate salutes and received a friendly nod from the woman they had once known as Ms Hickey, a teacher at a small school in country Australia.

Feeling intensely pleased with the developments, Josh followed Kyle and Greg out of the Captain's cabin

Chapter 16

The next two days were calm but intensely busy. Both young men worked long hours absorbing their new duties and saw little of each other except briefly in the Officers' Mess as they grabbed a quick meal.

And then the calm broke.

* * *

The warning sirens blared through the ship.

"ACTION STATIONS!" blasted from the various audio outlets. "THIS IS NOT A DRILL!"

Men and women began running in all directions as they went to their standard stations for emergency situations. There was little confusion, everybody knew exactly what to do, as did Josh who raced to the navigation control room and reported to his senior officer, Commander Rosshon. The Commander nodded at him but said nothing. Josh knew they had little to do until they received a clear command to go somewhere, but he checked all the computer screens and made sure he had the location of every nearby Wormhole fixed in his memory. It was a capability he had discovered to his astonishment at the Academy. Somehow, he was able to visualise the entire galaxy in his mind and work out the relationships of all the known Wormholes and how to use them to cross vast sections of space in a few seconds. He had studied the hugely complex process of calculating the exact speed and angle of approach to specific spots in a wormhole to travel to different parts of the Galaxy and somehow mastered with ease what took other people years to learn. His instructors had called it "genius" but it seemed simple to Josh.

The next message on the loudspeakers was a surprise.

"Mr Yshan, Mr Bradshaw, report to the Captain."

Josh looked at his Commander in surprise and received an equally surprised look in return.

"Go!" snapped the officer and Josh ran from the Navigation section.

He met Kyle outside the Captain's cabin.

"No idea," said Kyle in answer to Josh's unspoken question and they walked into the cabin.

She looked up and waved them in. "Watch," she said and turned to the large video screen against one wall. "This is what came in three minutes ago."

The face of the Fleet Admiral filled the screen.

"At 20:14, Yshan Galactic Standard Time, over four hundred alien space ships appeared in the home world quadrant. They came through Wormhole WBZ237 and surrounded Home World. Three of our Frigates who were in orbit attacked the alien fleet and were destroyed in seconds. All ships must now get away as rapidly as possible until we can prepare a battle plan. We have no idea of the source of these ships or their capabilities. I repeat, all ships, get away now, adopt Plan 52."

The image cut off and was replaced by a picture of a vast fleet of ships of quite unknown design. They were spherical and seemed to have no distinguishing characteristics.

"Nothing like we've ever seen before," the Captain said.

Josh realised he was holding his breath and slowly let it out.

"All right Josh, this where we need your genius," said the Captain. She seemed quite calm. "Any ideas?"

Josh calmed down and felt a wave of confidence run through him. He knew exactly what to do. "Yes, Ma'am," he said.

"How much time to prepare your plan?" she asked.

"About two hours."

"Good. Go. Get back here in two hours or less. Kyle, you understand the capacity of these new torpedoes?"

"Yes, Ma'am. They're astounding."

"Okay. Work with Josh, both of you get back here when you're ready."

The two young officers ran out of the cabin.

"My cabin," said Kyle. "I've got full computer power there."

"The privilege of royalty, eh?" said Josh and they moved rapidly. Josh knew exactly what to do.

Only ninety three minutes later, Josh hit the communications button.

"We're ready, Ma'am," he said.

"Get to the Bridge," came the terse command.

Two minutes later, they were in an area they rarely visited, the Command Deck, known in almost all Navies throughout the Universe as the Bridge. The Captain was sitting in her command chair, her First Officer on her left and to Josh's surprise, Greg Foster, Charlie's father was sitting on her other side.

"Tell me," snapped the Captain and Josh rapidly outlined his plan.

"And that works with you?" she said, turning to Kyle.

"Yes, Ma'am. It will work."

"Greg?" She turned to her right and Charlie's father nodded.

"Sounds about right," he said.

"Both of you, take your positions," the Captain said.

The two men stood a short distance apart, Josh at an immense video screen that had nothing but the outside image of the stars on it and Kyle at a similar screen that showed the status of every torpedo and weapon aboard.

"All hands, this is the Captain," said the woman in the Command Seat. "I am passing control of the Ship to Lieutenants Yshan and Bradshaw for a special commission. All officers will take their orders from these two until I say otherwise. Specifically, Commander Rosshon in Navigation, Commander Alleon in Armaments, do you both understand?"

"Understood, Captain," came the calm responses from both men. For just a second, Josh felt some amusement about how these very senior men would feel taking orders from two brand new officers, then smothered the thought. He had a job to do, as did they. He took a deep breath, looked sideways at Kyle and received a smile of encouragement.

"Navigation, steer for Wormhole NTS4591," he said. "Velocity at Point 95 Light."

"That will be eighteen minutes," came the immediate response.

"Noted," Josh answered and set his console timer.

For the next seventeen minutes, nobody said a word while the ship raced silently through space at ninety five percent of light speed until Josh broke the tense silence.

"Navigation, go to position fourteen hundred units from the wormhole, five hundred units above the central plane, zero from the horizontal."

"Fourteen hundred away, five hundred above, zero horizontal, aye," said the navigation officer.

Josh turned to the screen. The wormhole was a ring of fire that filled the screen, but superimposed on one section of the screen was a small red circle. Josh had calculated that position with his computer. From the ship's current position, it would hit the Wormhole at exactly the right angle and exactly the right speed to take it to a specific point in space many light years away.

"Helm, from the new position, steer for that circle at Point 371 Light."

"Point 371 Light, aye."

The ring of fire seemed to race towards the ship and then passed on all sides of it. There was blackness after they had passed through.

"Position check," snapped Josh.

"Dead on the projected position," replied the voice. "We are twenty-two hundred and eighteen light years from Yshan, in Quadrant 875."

"Thank you, Nav," said Josh. His confidence was flowing, the first stage had been successful. "Steer for Wormhole HJK9854, Point 891 Light."

"Wormhole HJK9854, Point 891 Light, aye," said the Navigator. "That will be forty-three minutes."

"Understood," said Josh and reset the console clock.

Forty four minutes later, the ship passed through the second wormhole at a point, in a direction and at a speed precisely calculated by Josh.

"Twelve thousand, one hundred and ninety seven light years from Yshan," said the Navigator. "Quadrant 9012."

"Wormhole MVC4554," said Josh. "Point 895 Light"

"Eight minutes," said Nav.

"Wormhole NYT7765," said Josh. "Point 814 Light."

"Fourteen minutes," said Nav.

The silence as the ship flew to its next transition point was abruptly broken.

"Captain, Helm."

"Yes, Helm," said the Captain.

"We're picking up a distress beacon. It's Yshan, coming from a planet in the Zucusti quadrant, thirty three light years from here."

"Noted, Helm. I'll send a ship there when this mission is complete."

"Yes, Ma'am," said the Helm officer.

The silent race to the Wormhole continued.

"One minute to Wormhole NYT7765."

"Thank you, Nav," said Josh. "Note your entrance details and follow."

"Noted and following."

Yet again, the ship rushed towards a huge ring of fire in which a small red dot had been placed on the screen.

"Seventy-two thousand light years from Yshan."

"Wormhole LPY6549," said Josh. "Point 886 Light."

"Twelve minutes."

"Thank you Nav. Kyle, get ready."

At last Kyle spoke. "Armaments?"

"Armaments, aye." A different voice responded.

"Arm all torpedoes. Prepare the spread and ignition times as per the details on the computer."

"Spread and times set."

"Thank you, Armaments," said Kyle and turned to Josh.

"Next wormhole?"

"Next wormhole," agreed Josh. "Nav, head for Wormhole BVC7801, Point 912 Light. Your target is set, take the path through it I've already preset. Do not acknowledge further orders."

"Armaments?" said Kyle. "On my mark, release all torpedoes."

"Understood, Lieutenant Yshan. On your mark."

"Battle stations," said the Captain calmly. "All hands prepare to engage the enemy. If this has worked as it seems, we have vanished from any detection possible by the Alien Fleet and we will appear without warning but within torpedo range."

The tension on the Bridge began rising as the final wormhole was approached.

The ring of fire rushed towards them and they hurtled through.

"Torpedoes, shoot!" said Kyle.

Nothing could be seen or felt, but in the distance, Josh saw the immense fleet of alien ships and his confidence seemed to shrink. There were hundreds of them! What if this didn't work?

"Well done, Josh," said the voice of Captain Sestucal. "We've come in behind them and they won't have time to respond before...."

In the distance, a series of tiny sparks lit up. Nothing else seemed to happen.

"Sensors!" snapped the Captain.

The first officer examined a screen at his side and grinned cheerfully. "All enemy ships are without power and weapons," he said. "Life support systems remain in operation."

Captain Sestucal let out a long slow breath. "Well done, Mr Yshan," she said. "That distribution and timing worked perfectly. Every ship in that fleet has been disabled."

"Thank you, Ma'am," Kyle said and grinned across at Josh.

"Congratulations, Greg," said the Captain. "Your torpedoes seem to have worked!"

"Always knew they would, skipper!" said Charlie's father. "I'm a genius, remember!"

The Captain laughed and looked like the young Ms Hickey again.

* * *

The shuttle moved slowly through the enemy fleet. The atmosphere was tense, everybody hiding their fear that perhaps the torpedoes hadn't worked completely and some ships might have weapons available.

But nothing happened.

Beside the shuttle pilot, the ship carried the Captain, Josh, Kyle and more than twenty armed troops carrying heavy weapons.

"Can you get in, Lieutenant?" the Captain asked.

"I think so, Ma'am," the pilot replied. "Sensors say that...." Without completing his sentence, a massive door slid sideways in the waist of the largest battleship that they had decided must be the command vessel in the fleet and the shuttle drifted inside and landed in a vast cavern, quite similar to the shuttle hangar on the Yshan ship.

"Atmosphere's good," said the pilot.

"Interesting," said the Captain. "They must come from a similar world to ours. Gravity seems about the same and if they can control gravity and wormhole navigation, they have a similar technology to ours. Anyway, let's go and find out. Full alert, everybody."

The door to the shuttle opened and the armed troops led the way, weapons at the ready.

"Clear!" shouted the troop commander and Captain Sestucal walked out, followed by Josh and Kyle.

They waited a few minutes and at last, people appeared. At the end of the hangar, a small group entered. Josh stared curiously. The arrivals looked human, perhaps taller than average, slimmer and they moved in a graceful manner as if underwater. The faces seemed quite human, though they had no noses, just two small holes where nostrils would be.

"I am Captain Sestucal of the Yshan Galactic Fleet," said the woman. "Can you understand me?"

There was no response from the aliens. One of them walked until it was standing just two metres from the Captain and the armed guards immediately raised their weapons and pointed at the alien group. None of them moved, and Josh, who was watching closely was unable to see if the immobility was because of shock, fear or incomprehension. The leader, for that was what Josh assumed, looked almost human, probably male and wore a garment resembling a set of blue overalls. A white stripe down the left side of the man's chest had various markings on it and Josh wondered if these denoted rank in some way.

But then came the surprise. Two more shapes appeared. They looked human. One was male and Josh remembered seeing that face years ago back on Earth. The other one was not familiar. The tall, slender young woman was quite beautiful, he thought, long dark hair falling down on her back, she was dressed in a royal blue, well-cut tunic.

"You'll need an interpreter until the computers learn the language," she said.

"Well, hello Sophie," said Kyle. "We were all wondering where you'd got to. You too, Uncle Omaron. So what have you two been up to the last five years?"

Chapter 17

Off duty, Kyle and Josh sat in the Officers' Lounge in the Battle Cruiser. They were both subdued after watching the alien crew members being led off under guard to a waiting freighter. Several such ships had been loaded with the crews of all the invader vessels, leaving each ship with just a skeleton crew. Their engines and weapons systems had all been made useless and a small platoon of armed troops took up residence in each ship.

"No idea where they came from?" asked Josh.

Kyle shook his head. "None. I think I have enough privilege to be told, but nobody's got any idea yet. Our boffins are taking their computers apart to track the route they took here, and I heard they're beginning to think they've crossed inter-galactic space."

"Holy duck-poo!" exclaimed Kyle. "That must mean wormholes that connect the galaxies! That opens up a lot of possibilities!"

"It does," agreed Kyle. "Meanwhile, the language computers are working on the prisoners and we should have translation capabilities soon."

"And what's happening to them meanwhile?" asked Josh.

"They're all being dropped on an island in the central ocean. There's shelter, food and supplies are being provided, but there's no chance of escape. Once we've got to the bottom of all this, they'll probably be sent home after the ships have been disarmed."

"Can I get you another coffee?" asked Josh. But before either of the boys could move, their personal communicators buzzed.

"Report to the Captain's cabin," said the soft voice.

"Belay that coffee," said Kyle with a grimace. "I think I know what this is about."

* * *

"Let me repeat your brother's question, Sophie," said the Captain. "Where have you been and what have you been doing the last five years since your exile ended?"

She sat behind the desk in her cabin and Sophie and her Uncle stood stiffly on their feet on the other side. Kyle, Josh and Greg sat in chairs against the wall. Josh could sense the distress in his friend as he watched his sister. It seemed an open and shut case of treason against the Empire and the penalty for that was life-time exile to the far reaches of the Galaxy.

"You've done well for yourself, Ms Hickey," said Sophie with a sneer. "I suppose having saved that little twit Henry to take MY throne has been a lot of help."

The Captain ignored the insolence. "How about you, Omaron Yshan? You want to be more informative?"

Omaron folded his arms in defiance. "Somebody had to do something about the Empire's safety," he said quietly. "Since we lost the last true Emperor, things started going downhill. This fool's parents..." he turned and pointed a finger at Kyle, "they were worse than useless. It was almost a certainty that the Star would appoint young Kyle next time and we both knew that would start the downfall."

The Captain smiled without humour. "And you decided you were wiser than the Star and would make the decisions instead?"

"Why not?" replied Omaron in an off-hand manner.

"Many have tried that before," said the Captain. "You should read your history. What happened to them?"

Omaron shrugged.

"They died in exile," chimed in Sophie. "They were never allowed within a hundred light years of Yshan again and they had to wear signal anklets to make sure."

For the first time she showed some expression and Josh was sure it was sadness.

"We're heading into home planet orbit," said the Captain. "A security team will take you down where you will both be held until your trial for Imperial Treason."

She was about to say more when a soft buzzer sounded.

"Yes, First Officer?" she said.

Josh decided she must be a lot angrier than she was letting on. He knew that normally she addressed her First Officer as Pelle, his first name.

"Orders from Fleet Command, Captain," said the First Officer. "Follow up on the emergency signal we picked up during the Grand Tour of the Galaxy that we were taken on by Lieutenant Bradshaw."

At last the Captain smiled. "Get us under way, Pelle," she said. She looked up at the two prisoners. "You two will be confined to a cell until we return home," she said.

The door opened and two armed troopers appeared. With no orders being given, they took the prisoners' arms and led them out of the cabin.

"A sad situation," said the Captain as she stood up and the other three murmured sounds of agreement before returning to their stations.

Chapter 18

The Battle Cruiser hung in orbit around a small, rocky planet.

"Unimpressive," muttered Kyle from the viewing screen.

"Atmosphere thin, but breathable," reported the Helm officer. "About equivalent to Yshan at three thousand metres. There is water and some vegetation, some small forests, local animals appear to present no danger."

"Have you located the beacon?" asked the Captain.

"Yes, Ma'am," the young woman at the helm replied. "It's on the coast of a major land mass, southern hemisphere, just under one thousand kilometres south of the equator. A moderate climate, maximum temperatures can reach twenty degrees, minimum temperatures down to minus fifteen."

"Not exactly a tropical paradise," Kyle murmured.

"Mr Bradshaw, Mr Yshan, here's your chance for action," said the Captain. "Take a shuttle, a platoon of troops, go and see who's down there, if anyone. Take weapons. Mr Yshan, you're in command."

"Yes, Ma'am," said the young officers in unison and moved rapidly to the shuttle hangar. They were met at the shuttle by the Chief Petty Officer who had greeted them on their arrival, but instead of his uniform, he had on full combat gear as did the ten men and women behind him. The CPO snapped a smart salute at Kyle.

"Troops ready for your order, sir," he said.

Kyle returned the salute. "Get the men aboard, Chief Petty Officer," he said. "Follow that beacon."

Two minutes later, the shuttle was in free fall towards the rocky surface of the planet. No orders were needed as the pilot followed his instruments down to the coast line a little south of the planet's equator and landed about a hundred metres from the spot indicated.

"Looks like wreckage, sir," said the pilot.

"I think that's a life pod from a Fleet ship," said Kyle. "What do you think, Mr Karlon?"

In their training at the Fleet Academy, they'd been taught quite thoroughly that Non Commissioned Officers, especially Chief Petty Officers really ran the military and no junior officer should ever be ashamed or reticent about asking the advice of one. It was quite common for a CPO to be addressed as "Mr" by all officers, regardless of rank.

"Indeed it is, sir," said the CPO. "I have no idea how it got so far out here, but that's an Yshan design, though it's a few years out of date. I believe it's a Mark V. We have Mark VIIIs on the ship now."

"We'd better go and have a look then," said Kyle. He wore a small blaster weapon at his side, as did Josh.

"Ready, men," called the CPO and Kyle pressed the button that opened the shuttle hatch. A blast of cool air greeted them, but it smelled clean, if a bit thin. Kyle jumped down to the ground, but Josh moved carefully down the steps, sensing less than average gravity on this small world. He would have to move carefully, though he knew the soldiers were all experienced in different conditions on a variety of worlds.

At the head of the troops but with the CPO alongside, they walked slowly to the metal heap. As they got closer, they realised the small shuttle was not much damaged at all, just tilted a few degrees on its side where it had come to rest.

"Bit of a crash landing," said Josh. "Must have been the last of their fuel. But maybe they've survived it."

They reached the small ship and surrounded it, weapons at the ready.

Josh noted the serial number on the prow of the wreck and pressed his communications button.

"Helm," said the young officer on the ship.

"Jennie, track this serial number," Josh said, and read out the six digits.

"That will take a while, Josh. I'll call you when I find it."

"Thank you," said Josh and watched as two troopers cautiously approached and prised open the door to the pod. They peered in and raised their heads.

"Clear, sir," one said.

"Spread out, see if we can see any tracks," said Kyle.

"Er.. no need, sir," said CPO Karlon and pointed. Only a few hundred metres away, two people had appeared from behind a hill. They walked slowly towards the waiting troops and stopped just a few metres away.

One was a man. He was quite old, his hair was a messy length down his back and his face showed the ravages of a hard scrabble for life. The second shape was a woman with a similarly coarse appearance.

"I was wondering when somebody would show up," the man said. "You've really taken your time. We need to go home."

It was the Chief Petty Officer who finally understood. He snapped a perfect salute at the man.

"Your Majesty, Emperor Garamax the Eighteenth, I'm delighted we've found you. We all thought you were dead. This is your nephew Kyle Yshan."

* * *

The ride back to the Battle Cruiser took place in silence. Beyond a direct stare at Kyle, the old Emperor had said nothing to him and ignored him throughout the short walk to the shuttle and the take off.

Josh's mind was in a whirl. Was this *really* the old Emperor who was supposed to have died in a deliberate torpedo hit on his ship while observing war games with the Fleet? If so, what did that do to Henry's position? Could this man reclaim the throne? Would the Star approve? And why was he so obviously hostile to Kyle? He tried to catch Kyle's eye but his friend stayed in the co-pilot's seat for the approach to the Cruiser and said nothing.

The shuttle entered the main hangar and the door opened.

"Your Majesty, I'll take you to see the Captain," said Kyle.

"No you won't," snapped the old man. "First, you'll take us to a cabin where we can clean up and find new clothing. When I'm ready, I'll go and see the Captain. Don't you think I know my way around a Fleet Cruiser?"

Josh was shocked at the rudeness, but said nothing. Kyle simply nodded.

The CPO broke in, obviously seeing the hostility between the two men. "I'll show you to the guest quarters, Your Majesty," he said and led off with the implicit assumption that the old couple would follow. They did, sensing the authority in the man.

"What the heck's going on?" muttered Josh to Kyle.

"I have no idea," replied Kyle, traces of anger showing in his face. "Obviously, I never knew him but I'd never heard that he was a bad-tempered old fool like that! My father thought the world of him."

"That was an ugly performance," said Josh.

"Too right," agreed Kyle. "We'd better report to the Captain."

"There's something wrong about this whole thing," said Josh as they made their way to the Bridge. "Lots of questions."

"You're right," said Kyle. "Let's wait till we see the skipper."

A few minutes later, they entered the Bridge where the Captain and the First Officer were standing by the communications screen. The face on the screen was of the Fleet Admiral.

"And where are they now?" asked the Admiral.

"They insisted on being taken to guest quarters, sir," replied Captain Sestucal.

"All right, I've no doubt they'd want to clean up before talking to anyone. You'll make sure they get adequate food, anything they want?"

"Of course, sir. What happens next?"

"A good question," the Admiral said. "We've advised the Emperor but I'm quite certain nothing will change. Garamax the Nineteenth will remain our Emperor. The

Star would never have proclaimed him if it had not been the true path. Let me know when you've spoken to them. But head for Yshan, maximum rate."

"Yes, sir," said the Captain and the screen went dark. "Pelle, take us home, as fast as this old tub can make it," she said to the First Officer and turned to see the two young men at the entrance to the Bridge.

"My ready room, gentlemen," she said and led the way into the cabin next to the Bridge that was used by the Commander when needing to stay close to developments. Inside was a pleasantly laid-out room with a large desk, several video screens and a social area of several armchairs surrounding a coffee table. The Captain took a seat and gestured to the two men to do the same.

"Report, Mr Yshan," she said.

"It appears to be exactly what it seems, Ma'am," replied Kyle. "That pod is a Mark V, some thirty years older than the current Mark VIIIs we have. The serial number checks with the ship on which the Emperor and Empress were watching the war games when a rogue torpedo destroyed it."

"And these are definitely your Aunt and Uncle?"

"To be honest Ma'am, I can't be certain. I've only seen pictures of them before their disappearance, but that was twenty five years ago. Given what they've gone through on that rough little planet, it's reasonable that they'd look a lot different."

"That does sound reasonable, Mr Yshan. Mr Bradshaw, what about you? Do you have any concerns about this?"

"I do, Ma'am. I've read the reports of that accident, it's standard reading at the Academy. The torpedo that struck the ship was a Phalanx Mark IV. It was supposed to be a blank that would stop and be recovered later for analysis, but it had a functioning warhead. That has always been put down to a murderous plot against the Emperor."

"But..." prodded the Captain.

"The problem is, Ma'am," continued Josh, "a Phalanx warhead would have destroyed the ship instantly, in fact, *vaporised* it, and that's exactly what it did according to the reports at the time. Nobody would have stood any chance of getting to a life-pod after the strike, never mind get away a safe distance."

"You're the weapons expert, Mr Yshan, is that a correct conclusion?"

Despite his anger and tension, Kyle grinned at his friend. "The kid's got it right Ma'am! There should have been nothing at all remaining of the ship."

"And so...?" The Captain was testing the two young officers.

"They were expecting the strike, Ma'am," said Kyle. "They knew it was coming and they got into a life pod well before and pulled away from the ship in plenty of time to get clear."

"Did anyone see that?" asked the Captain.

"I suspect there was such a state of shock around the fleet that nobody even thought to look, Ma'am," replied Kyle.

The Captain's face was calm, but a tightness round her eyes indicated the shock she was feeling.

"So what you are saying, Mr Yshan, is that the Galactic Emperor feigned his own death and vanished. Can you think of any possible reason why he should do that?"

"No Ma'am, the whole idea is insane. I can't think of any possible reason why he'd so such a thing."

"Didn't the Star disappear at the same time?" asked Josh. "And the prince was kidnapped also?"

"That's so, Mr Bradshaw," said the Captain. "What bearing could that have on it?"

"I don't know, Ma'am," said Josh, uncomfortable under her strong gaze. "But all three events occurred at the same time. None of this makes sense to me."

"Nor me," the Captain replied. "But is there anything else that makes no sense?"

"Where we found them," said Josh. "That also makes no sense. There's no wormhole anywhere near the site of the war games. And to get to where they were would have required two transits through two different wormholes at speeds that are simply impossible for a life pod, never mind the time taken to reach even the first one. Pods just don't have that sort of engine."

The Captain looked searchingly at him.

"You're certain of that, Mr Bradshaw?"

"Yes, Ma'am. The nearest wormhole to that location would have taken twenty three minutes at Point Nine Light and even if they'd got there, which is impossible, there is no transit possible to where we found them without a second wormhole."

The Captain smiled briefly. "This is why I requested both of you to be assigned to my ship," she said. "You've proved your value. We seem to have a horrible problem."

"Ma'am, if I can suggest, keep the old Emperor under close observation," said Kyle. "There's something very wrong about this whole situation."

"Your advice is noted," the Captain said with a small smile. "Let's see what happens when His Majesty decides to come and talk to me. Meanwhile, go to Records at Fleet

Headquarters, obtain every known visual record of the destruction of that ship. Do it privately in your cabin, use my name as authorisation. See if you can find anything new."

"Yes, Ma'am," they replied in unison, stood up, replaced their uniform hats and gave a smart salute. She nodded and watched them leave the cabin.

* * *

The Captain was back on the Bridge when the old Emperor finally walked in three hours later, alone. He had bathed, shaved and found a tunic that fitted him. There were no badges of rank on the sleeves or shoulders but fresh marks showed where they had been cut away. The Captain kept a straight face.

"You have the Bridge, Pelle," she said softly. "Tell the boys." She winked at him. "Good afternoon, Your Majesty," she said to the old man. Let's go to my ready room." She led the way to the room that she had used to talk to Kyle and Josh. Inside, she stood and waited while the other selected a seat and sat down, then she did the same.

He glared at her as if he felt she should have remained standing, but wasted no time. "I demand that you take me back to Yshan immediately," he said.

"We have been underway at maximum speed since you came aboard," she said. "We have already made a transit through the first of three wormholes and we should make orbit round Yshan in approximately two hours."

"You will then take me down to the Capital."

She inclined her head. "Of course, Your Majesty."

"Get me in contact with the Emperor," he said. "Who is the Emperor, anyway? Which of my useless relatives has taken my throne?"

"Your son, Garamax," she replied, watching him closely. "He is the Nineteenth of that name."

The old man hid it well, but seemed startled. "My son? But..." He stopped and seemed thoughtful.

Watching on the screen in Kyle's cabin, Kyle took a sudden breath. "That hit him sideways," he murmured.

"He wasn't expecting it," agreed Josh. "And yet that's exactly what he should have expected."

"But what?" inquired Captain Sestucal.

The old man glared angrily at her. "You will continue to address me as 'Your Majesty' and you will stand in my presence. I am the Emperor of the Galaxy!"

"Actually, no, you're not," she replied and remained seated, looking him firmly in the eye as an equal. "The Emperor of the Galaxy, proclaimed by the Star, confirmed by the Golden Mask and beloved of the people is your son, Garamax the Nineteenth. Until the Star says otherwise, that's how it will remain."

"You have the Star?" he said loudly.

"Should that be in any doubt?" she asked. "Why would we not have the Star?"

"Oopsie!" said Josh. "He should not know anything about the Star's disappearance after his death. He's digging himself deeper and deeper into a very ugly hole."

As if realising his error, the old man went quiet for a moment.

"Get me the Emperor," he said suddenly and loudly, as if he could make the Captain obey his royal authority.

"I'm sorry, sir," she said firmly. "A communications blackout is in force, Fleet Admiral's orders. He feels that any leak about your return could cause unrest. This entire episode will remain secret until we can consult the Star."

"See that?" said Josh in excitement. "That scared the living daylights out of him! He doesn't want to consult the Star. I wonder why?"

"I think because he knows it won't let him take back the throne," said Kyle.

In the Captain's cabin, the old Emperor was looking severely agitated.

"This Cruiser has an Admiral's Stateroom," he said loudly. "I will take over that until we get to Yshan. And when we get there, I insist that the Imperial Shuttle is sent to collect me."

"No sir," replied the Captain. "You will remain in the guest quarters for the duration of the flight and when we hit orbit, several of my men will escort you to the standard shuttle and you will be taken to the Palace to meet the Emperor."

The man stared at her. "Are you telling me I'm under arrest? How dare you, Captain! I'll have you broken to Lieutenant for that!"

"Not under arrest, sir," Captain Sestucal replied. "It's protective custody until we can sort out everything. This is for your safety. However, I must advise you that your niece, Sophie is also aboard and she most certainly *IS* under arrest and will accompany you down to the planet when we reach orbit. She will not be sharing the comforts that you will have, as she remains in a cell, as does your younger brother, Omaron. There is much to discover, it seems."

"You have Omaron in a cell?" Garamax looked shocked.

"Yes, sir. Do you wish to speak to him or to your niece?"

Defeated and clearly broken, the Emperor shook his head, suddenly looking ten years older and meekly allowed himself to be taken back to his cabin.

The Captain looked up to where the invisible camera was located in the corner. "What do you think, gentlemen?"

"It's getting dirtier by the minute, Captain," Kyle replied. "Wasn't it strange that he didn't bother to ask why Omaron was under arrest?"

"I agree," she said. "Did you get those records?"

"Coming through in five minutes, Ma'am," said Josh.

"Good. Get to work. I want answers before we make planetfall on Yshan."

"Yes, Ma'am," acknowledged Josh and cut the connection.

Kyle and Josh sat back to wait for all the recordings of the tragedy that had killed the Emperor twenty five years ago.

Chapter 19

Even after seeing these recordings many times at the Academy, it was still hard for the two young officers to watch them again.

At hugely slowed rate, they watched the torpedo approach the Battle Cruiser as it sat a little away from the main body of the fleet.

"We never were able to track backwards and see where it came from," said Josh. "That's always been a huge mystery to me."

"To everyone," said Kyle. "We've backtracked its path a thousand times, it just seemed to come from nowhere."

"Can we have a look at that nowhere?"

"Sure." Kyle focused the computer and they watched the torpedo reverse its position over several thousand kilometres.

"There!" said Kyle. "It just appeared and howled off to the royal cruiser."

"Can you amplify that location?"

Kyle touched the controls and the picture grew larger, but seemed totally uninformative. One moment the space was vacant, the next the torpedo appeared and set off on its fatal course.

"How long did we have the royal ship in sight?" asked Josh.

"Pretty well all the time," replied Kyle. "Standard security."

"All right, can we focus on it from the beginning, say fifteen minutes before it was destroyed?"

"Yes, no problem."

The cruiser filled the screen.

"And the life pod would exit just there, is that right?" asked Josh, pinpointing a spot in the centre of the enormous ship.

"Same design as this one," said Kyle.

"Okay, let's amplify the escape pod hatch and then watch."

The picture changed and the focus became the hatchway from which the life pod would leave if one would go before the ship exploded.

"Hey!" said Kyle suddenly. "Look at that!"

In the screen, a tiny dot appeared as the hatch opened briefly. It flew at right angles from the ship and then.... vanished.

"What the...?" said Josh. "It looks like it was just covered by something!"

"Very strange," agreed Kyle. "Let's examine that area more closely."

Carefully, he enhanced the picture and they stared at the screen as the location was enlarged.

"Good grief, look at that!" shouted Josh in excitement. "The stars! They've been blocked by something."

Kyle saw it also. "There's a ship there! It's cloaked!"

Carefully, he focused more and more closely and finally they saw what was there.

"It's circular," said Kyle. "Or spherical, anyway. Somehow it's cloaked itself and it picks up the life pod."

They looked at each other.

"The alien ships are spherical," murmured Kyle.

"We'd better talk to the Captain," said Josh. "It looks like we know what happened."

"This is getting ugly in the extreme," murmured Kyle as he hit the communications button.

Chapter 20 – 25 Years Ago

"Garamax, you must attend the Star."

The soft voice broke through the Emperor's disturbed sleep and woke him. This was a rare but not unknown event, that the Star would awaken Emperor Garamax the Eighteenth, Lord of the entire Galactic Yshan Empire. Only three times had it happened during his six-year reign, each time to advise him of a personal crisis or an upcoming problem somewhere within his Empire. Moving carefully to avoid disturbing his young wife, he rose, donned a dressing gown and walked out of his room. The two guards who stood outside the door saluted, hiding their astonishment. In an Empire that had been peaceful for some centuries, an Emperor's appearance at night was almost unheard of.

The Chamber of the Star was down the corridor. Acknowledging the salutes, Garamax walked down to the Chamber and opened the door. The light came on automatically and Garamax stopped, as always awestruck by the scene. A large block of basalt, a metre tall and about the same wide and deep stood in the middle of the Chamber. On it lay the Star, the mysterious crystal that had guided the Yshan Family for five thousand years, leading them from a small, declining tribe on a world dying of hunger to the head of a Galactic Empire that was peaceful, prosperous and unchallenged. The crystal glowed with a faint light that waxed and waned every few seconds.

"Welcome, Emperor Garamax the Eighteenth," said the soft voice in his head.

"Why have you called me?" he asked.

"To advise you that your rule must end," said the voice.

"WHAT?" Garamax felts his legs go weak and he sat down on the rich carpet.

"This has never happened before in five thousand years. But you have changed, Garamax. The man we proclaimed six years ago is not the man we see here and you are no longer fit for rule."

Garamax felt anger rising in him.

"And just what is it that I have done that brings you to this conclusion?" he said loudly.

"The fact that you must ask that question is one of the problems. But you must know that the famine on the world of Hinores resulted in the deaths of thousands, despite the availability of huge amounts of food from nearby worlds. Your own advisors told you what needed to be done, you ignored them."

"The people of Hinores are no supporters of Yshan," snapped Garamax. "They mock me, they ignore our rules. Why should I help them?"

"Again, that tells us why you are no longer fit to rule. With power comes responsibility and the fact that you let thousands die out of a sense of superiority and personal pride is the problem. There have been similar episodes."

"That's not enough to remove an Emperor from the Throne!" shouted Garamax.

"You are no longer Emperor," said the soft voice. "You will bring your brother here tomorrow with witnesses and we will show our decision. It must be done at once because we are about to enter our period of silence."

Garamax stared at the crystal. He knew that the Star's hibernation period was due to begin soon, something that occurred every four hundred years when the Star went dormant for several weeks. The Star would soon be silent and unresponsive. A plan began to form in his mind. Without another word, he left the room.

No chunk of crystal was going to take the Galactic Throne away from him.

"Omaron, this will make a rich man of you," said Garamax.

The Emperor's youngest brother looked steadily at him. "You really intend to go ahead with this?"

"Do you think I'd let that idiot soft brother of ours become Emperor?" snapped Garamax. "He'd let the Empire fall apart!"

"I remember when all three of us met the Star as children," said Omaron. "Our father had died the day before. I remember I lifted the Star and nothing happened. Karocarl was next and it glowed quite brightly, but nothing to what happened when you raised it."

"It was a remarkable sensation," said Garamax thoughtfully. "Even though it had been expected as the eldest son has most often taken over the Throne, it was still astounding."

"It was a slap in the face for me," said Omaron in anger. "Have you any idea how embarrassing that was, in front of all those dignitaries, that dumb bit of crystal rejected me totally? Did you hear some of the giggles round the room? I wanted to die."

"It was astonishing," agreed Garamax. "It normally glows to some extent when any member of the Yshan family holds it. I felt sorry for you."

Omaron's face was still ugly with the memory. "Okay, so I have no reason to love the Star. Tell me the plan."

"We somehow feign my death," said Garamax. "Just as the Star goes dormant, I seem to get killed. They can't get the Star to endorse a new Emperor, so they'll make our brother Karocarl the temporary Emperor until the Star wakes up. But during that time, you steal the Star and hide it somewhere a really long way away. You take my son as well. I don't want the Star deciding he's the next Emperor until I'm ready to retire. And then when I'm found, safe and well, I naturally take the Throne back and as the Star is missing, nobody's going to object. Meanwhile, everybody will be so hysterical about some enemy plot, it will give me the opportunity to clamp down on the people a bit. Got it?"

"Got it. And what am I supposed to get out of it?"

"You'll be a hero all over the Galaxy for rescuing me and you can have pretty well anything you want."

Omaron sat back in seat thinking deeply. Finally, he spoke.

"I think I know how to do it," he said.

Three days later, Omaron came to see his brother.

"The Galactic Fleet will begin training war games in two days," he said. "You request to be on a cruiser to observe, and as an ex Fleet Officer, that will be seen as quite normal and the Admiral will be delighted. We've recently developed cloaking technology for space ships, it's already installed on my personal transport. When I send you the signal, you and your wife will enter a life pod and eject. I'll pick you up and get you away and then send a torpedo to destroy the cruiser. Two days later, I'll claim that I found you and bring you home to a triumphant return to reclaim the throne."

"Sounds good," said Garamax. "I didn't know about that cloaking technology. When did that happen?"

"Very recently and it's still secret. Has the Star gone dormant yet?"

"Twelve hours ago," said Garamax.

"Then I'll remove it tonight. As an Yshan family member, I have access to the Chamber."

Garamax nodded. "Do it," he said.

Omaron left the room and held his grin of triumph until nobody could see him.

Two days later, with the Emperor on the Battle Cruiser "Garamax XII," Omaron left Yshan and was picked up by an alien spaceship of a species that he had met while working on a remote planet at the far edge of the Galaxy. Fully cloaked, the ship approached the Yshan Galactic Fleet and picked up a tiny life pod that had left the Cruiser and then accelerated to light speed immediately. Although the departure was noted by the Yshan ship's crew, they only had a few seconds before a Phalanx Torpedo released by a second alien ship, also cloaked, blew the Battle Cruiser into dust.

Within the life pod, Emperor Garamax the Eighteenth and his wife waited impatiently for Omaron to come and release them. But the alien ship continued its high speed travel and passed through two different wormholes before the hatch door opened and the little life pod was released close to a small, barren planet over thirteen thousand light years from Yshan.

Only then did Garamax realise he had been betrayed by his brother.

Omaron returned to his own transport and departed the alien ship together with the dormant Star and the infant son of the Emperor.

He had his own plans for the Galactic Throne.

Chapter 21 – The Present

Henry stared at the elderly couple walking into the reception area.

"These are my parents?" he muttered uncertainly to Kyle and Josh standing by his side.

"They are, Henry," said Kyle. "But you must remember, they've been living a hard-scrabble existence alone on a hostile, barren planet for twenty five years."

"They don't look too pleased to see me."

"They were pretty crabby when they saw me, Henry. I don't think he likes being an *EX*-Emperor at all."

"That is the case, Sire," added Captain Sestucal. "I briefed you on my meeting with them."

"You did, Captain, but the reality is still ugly."

The old Garamax and his wife walked stiffly to the conference table where the rest were sitting and they all rose to their feet as the couple reached them. Henry walked out from the head of the table and went to greet them.

"Father, Mother, this wonderful..." he began, but the old man glared furiously at him.

"You will abdicate the throne immediately," he said in almost a snarl. "I will resume my position as Garamax the Eighteenth and you can go back to whatever backwater slum you came from."

A shocked silence lasted just a few seconds.

"I think not," said Henry, gave both his parents a cold stare and resumed his seat at the head of the table. Garamax began stamping after him.

"That's MY seat!" he shouted but was stopped by both Kyle and the Captain before he could take a few steps.

Garamax was furious. "Get these people out of my way!" he roared, spit flying from his lips. "What are they doing in here, anyway? Who authorised them? That woman has already had the audacity to question me aboard one of my own ships of the Imperial Fleet. I demand that she be removed."

"She stays," said Henry. "And I authorised everyone to be here, I, Garamax the Nineteenth, Emperor of the Yshan Galactic Empire. Do you question my authority?"

Josh almost laughed with delight. The power and charisma of his old friend was astonishing, a far cry from the scrawny little nine-year old boy he had known at school on Earth. This was the first time he had seen Henry exercise his authority and it exhilarated him.

Garamax had not given up. "I DO question it," he shouted. "I am the rightful Emperor and now that I've been found again, I will resume my throne."

"Ah, well, that's all questionable," said Henry. He smiled, but watching him, Josh thought that he would never wish to be on the receiving end of a smile like that. It indicated great danger. Henry nodded at the Captain. "Will you explain to my parents, Captain?"

"I'd be delighted, Sire," she replied. She gestured at the old couple. "Would you take your seats, please?"

Appearing to sense the situation and their total loss of authority, Garamax and his wife took seats at the bottom of the table. A huge three-dimensional image appeared in the middle of the room. The scene was in space and focused on the enormous battle cruiser in the centre, while several other ships floated in the vicinity.

"This is the official recording of the Fleet War Games of twenty five years ago," said the Captain. "The battle cruiser is the "Garamax XII" in which you and your wife, the Empress were observing. Please observe."

The tiny spark of the torpedo was barely seen when the battle cruiser exploded into dust. Despite having seen this many times while at the Academy and then again just days before when he and Kyle reviewed it, Josh still flinched with horror.

"As you see," continued the Captain. "That was a Phalanx IV missile which destroyed the ship instantaneously, killing over four hundred Fleet Officers and crew."

Despite her cold, even tones, Josh detected a trace of anger in her voice.

"And yet," said the Captain, "you and your lady wife are with us, twenty five years later, having been rescued by my ship off a planet over twelve thousand light years away having crash landed in a life pod from the cruiser that had been destroyed. Can you explain how that happened, sir?"

Garamax stared back at her. "I was rescued by another ship," he said, tension making his voice crack.

"Well, you see sir, that presents us with two problems," said the Captain. "Leaving aside the third question of where did that torpedo originate, the first problem is how did you have time to get to a life pod and get away? The second is who picked you up?"

"We were touring the life pod bay," retorted the old man defiantly. "We were lucky and were able to get into a pod and escape."

The Captain shook her head. "You were once a Fleet Officer, sir," she said. "A very fine one, by all accounts, including my father's recollections. You know the capabilities of a Phalanx IV torpedo. It took one fifteenth of a second to vaporise the Cruiser and all its crew. My father was Navigation Officer on the ship, by the way."

For several seconds, she and Garamax stared at each other.

"You must have had considerable warning to make your escape," the Captain continued. "And you had a ship standing by to pick you up."

Garamax said nothing, but the slump in his shoulders indicated his awareness of his defeat.

"Interesting thing about that ship." The Captain pointed at the image in the room. "Watch."

In an intense silence, the people in the room watched the tiny shape of the life pod move rapidly away from the doomed battle cruiser and then... vanish.

"Let's amplify that image and slow it down," said the Captain. "You will see that there is actually a shape blocking out the stars just where the pod disappears. We'd never seen that before because everybody naturally assumed you had died with ship and we didn't investigate until these young officers studied the recordings. It's time you told us what happened, sir."

Garamax was now completely broken.

"Omaron said his ship was equipped with new cloaking technology," he mumbled.

"Cloaking technology? The Empire is only now developing cloaking technology," the Captain interrupted. "We certainly didn't have it twenty five years ago. So where do you think that ship came from?"

Garamax was looking confused. "I don't understand," he muttered. "Omaron said..."

"Omaron?" broke in Kyle. "My uncle, your youngest brother after my father? He's part of this?"

Garamax didn't look at him.

Kyle looked across at the Captain. "That would seem to explain a great deal, Ma'am," he said.

She nodded and turned to Henry. "I agree with Lieutenant Yshan, Sire," she said.

"Indeed," said Henry. "Continue, Captain."

"Thank you, Sire." She turned her attention back to Garamax. "Let me show you something else, sir," she said. "This has been kept from you while you were aboard my ship and before this moment, but this is what happened before we came to find you."

The three dimensional scene in the room changed to a view of the alien fleet that had invaded the Empire.

"Several hundred alien ships appeared through a wormhole near Yshan while most of our fleet was dispersed on patrols around the Galaxy. They destroyed several of our ships. The ships appear identical to the one that picked you up and now that our scientists have inspected some of them, it appears they do have cloaking ability. We defeated the aliens with the tactical skills of these two young men here and technology developed by a most brilliant man who is the father-in-law of your nephew, Kyle."

Garamax didn't look away from the scene of the alien fleet.

"So what we must consider, sir," continued the Captain, "is that you and your brother conspired to spirit you away for some reason and that the kidnapping of your son and the removal of the Star during its dormant phase are also involved."

Garamax looked white and Josh could see that he was trembling.

"I didn't know anything about any aliens," he stammered. "Omaron said we had cloaking technology and he'd bring me back after a few days."

"But why?" demanded the Captain. "What possible logic is there behind all this?"

Garamax shook his head and stared down at the table, saying nothing.

The room was silent and everybody looked at Henry.

"So, father," he said, looking to the end of the table. "You still persist in your claim to the throne? How about we take it to the Final Authority?"

Garamax flinched. "No need for that," he muttered.

"Ah, but I insist," said Henry, the same cold, dangerous smile on his lips. He stood up and everybody in the room followed suit. The image of the battle scene faded and vanished. Henry led the way out of the room and down the corridor to the Chamber of the Star. Kyle and the Captain stayed close to the old couple and Josh brought up the rear, suddenly nervous. He had not seen the Star since the ceremony when Henry had held it up before the thousands of people in the city square and for billions of watchers throughout the Galaxy and he had never been in this legendary Chamber.

Henry stopped before the big bronze doors to the Chamber, touched the panel and it opened. He walked in and stopped before the black basalt block on which the Star rested. It was pulsing with a low stream of light.

Josh stayed by the wall nearest the door. He felt a little breathless, sensing the power in the room and the huge fear radiating from the old Garamax.

He watched Henry as he raised the Star to waist level. The glow increased a fraction and Henry nodded to Kyle. "Time you tried this again, Kyle," he said with a friendly smile.

Without any obvious emotion, Kyle took the glowing crystal, stared down at it for a few moments then raised it above his head.

The glow increased considerably but not to the level of the immense blaze that Josh had seen before. Kyle lowered it with a slight sigh of relief and handed it back to Henry.

Henry laughed. "Not yet your turn, Kyle," he said.

"And I hope it never is, Sire," said Kyle. "That's never been the path I wanted."

"I know it." Henry smiled again and turned to Garamax, his face turning cold.

"Your turn, father," he said. "Who knows, the Star may validate your claim."

Looking frightened, Garamax stepped closer and reluctantly took the crystal. Almost immediately, the glow faded to a barely detectible gleam.

"Not looking good, Father," said Henry. "But you know what to do next."

Garamax slowly raised the crystal above his head, staring up with wide, terrified eyes.

Nothing happened. Garamax stayed frozen for a few seconds then lowered the Star, silently handed it back to

Henry and stepped back to join his wife who was quietly weeping by the wall.

Henry held the Star briefly at waist level then firmly raised it above his head.

The Star blazed with the light of the entire Galaxy.

Unable to help himself, Josh sank to his knees, aware that all the watchers in the room did the same.

"That seems to settle that," said Henry and replaced the Star on the basalt block as the light faded to normal levels.

As the observers got back to their feet, the Star emitted a brief high-pitched noise and a brilliant, pure blue beam of light flashed out to where the old couple were standing.

Without a sound, old Garamax collapsed. Josh who was nearest, stepped to the huddled shape and checked his heart and pulse. He looked up at Henry, his face white.

"Your father is dead, Sire," he said.

Chapter 22 – Thirty Two Years Earlier

Omaron Yshan watched the coronation of his oldest brother Garamax the Eighteenth with a sour feeling of complete failure in his soul. He had always been the weakest of the three brothers, he know that. Neither as tall and handsome as Garamax, or as athletic and academically brilliant as the middle brother, Karocarl, both of whom had been accepted by The Fleet Academy which granted no places on the basis of station in life, only ability, Omaron had achieved nothing memorable.

Their father, the Emperor had always tried to avoid showing favouritism to his sons, but Omaron had always seen the delight on the Emperor's face when he greeted his two eldest sons and though he had tried to hide it, Omaron had seen the slight expression of disappointment with Omaron. It had knotted his guts into painful centres of rage and envy.

The worst moment of his life had been the day his father died. Not for any grief at the loss of a parent, but for the final rejection which he knew was coming. It still caused flaming rage and pain in his heart when he thought of it.

The three sons of the dead Emperor, Harlamon the Sixth filed into the Chamber of the Star, followed by the Fleet Admiral, the General of the Planetary Forces and the three senior advisors to the Emperor's Court of Imperial Management. This court, with fifteen other advisors, the greatest minds in the Empire provided the management of the planets within the Galactic Empire.

In the centre of the Chamber stood the metre high block of black basalt on which the Star lay. It glowed with a light that could have lit a ballroom, maybe aware of what was to happen, but nobody knew if the Star felt emotions or anything else. Omaron felt a mix of awe, rage and hatred directed at the glowing crystal on the plinth. It would decide the next Emperor. He knew it would be Garamax, it was almost always the eldest child of the Emperor, though Omaron knew that variations to the norm had occurred in the past. The second daughter of Harlamon the First had been proclaimed by the Star over thirty-three hundred years ago to become Empress Leonie the First. Four hundred years later, the youngest son of Garamax the Twelfth, had become Karocarl the Third and once, the Star had by-passed the existing line and chosen the youngest brother of the Emperor to succeed him.

So despite his ugly emotions, Omaron retained a glimmer of tiny hope. Maybe the Star would recognise something in him that would make him superior to his brothers' looks, brilliance and leadership talents and proclaim him Emperor.

As the youngest, he was the first to be offered the Star.

"Prince Omaron Yshan," called the Senior Advisor of the Imperial Court. Omaron had never bothered to learn the woman's name. He stepped forward to the plinth and the short, powerfully-built woman, reputed to be the finest mathematician in the Empire lifted the Star and placed it in his hands. He stood frozen, afraid to take the next step.

"Lift it up," the woman urged and Omaron forced himself to raise the large crystal above his head. The strong light that had been there faded almost to nothing, barely a gleam in its centre. Trembling, Omaron lowered it, aware of the tiny smile of derision on the woman's face and hearing some barely smothered snorts of laughter from others in the room.

Losing all control of himself, Omaron ran out of the Chamber, tears of rage and embarrassment running down his cheeks.

Only later did he learn that his oldest brother, as expected, had been proclaimed by the Star as Emperor Garamax the Eighteenth. Unable to live with the mockery of the family and courtiers, he left Yshan in his personal cruiser within an hour of the coronation and fled the Empire.

* * *

Four years later, he had found his way to a lightly populated planet with little industry and vast, empty territories. He was not short of resources, being a royal prince of the richest planet in a wealthy Empire and he had the technology within his ship to build a fine house by a lake some hundred kilometres from the small town that supplied his needs. The life pod from his ship provided transportation but he rejected any communication systems, having no wish to read about the brilliant leadership of his eldest brother from the throne that he so desperately wanted for himself. Otherwise he kept his own company and nursed his bitterness alone.

The shock that ran through him when the small ship landed on his property just a hundred metres from the house was immense. Trembling, gasping for breath, he opened his cupboard and extracted the heavy blaster rifle, slung it over his shoulder and strapped a pistol to his belt. He watched from the window for several minutes before a hatch opened in the ship and two people got out. They seemed to be carrying no weapons that he could see, but his fear didn't decrease.

They walked the short distance towards the house. There was something odd about the motion, Omaron thought, they seemed to be very tall, well above normal height and walked with a strange flowing movement. They stopped a few metres from the building and held their hands up high, the universal gesture of peace and a signal that they held no weapons. Breathing a little easier, Omaron checked his weapons again and walked outside.

For a moment, he studied the two people. They looked normal, apart from the odd gait, their faces looked standard. But something niggled at Omaron's mind, something about the faces was not right, there seemed no mobility of the features whatever, as if the faces were masks of some sort.

He stared at them and still they didn't speak.

"I think the traditional phrase is, "We come in peace," said Omaron, trying to ease his fear with a small joke. "Do you?"

"We do," replied one, but while his lips moved, something didn't look real and Omaron decided he'd heard the faintly artificial sound of a computer translator. So these people had not learned the Galactic standard Yshan language by direct computer transfer as all citizens of the Empire did in childhood. They had not come from within the Empire. A small twinge of fear and excitement ran through him. *What did this make possible?*

"Then why are you here? And where are you from?" he asked.

"We are here because we can help each other."

"How?"

"A trade," said the alien and now Omaron was sure. These were not one of the known races in the Galactic Empire. There had always been the possibility that an intelligent species with high technology would one day be discovered somewhere in a Galaxy that was still a long way short of being fully explored, but after several thousand years of Empire, it had never happened.

"What sort of trade?" He was feeling more confident now. There was something happening that he sensed would be of benefit to him.

"You want the throne," said the other.

Omaron gasped audibly in shock. *How did they know? What else did they know?*

"In return for what?"

"Some of your planets. Some of your wealth. Yours is an empire rich beyond belief. Ours is short of many things."

"Your *EMPIRE?*" Omaron's sense of shock increased sharply. "There's another empire within the Galaxy and we have never found it?"

"Not within the Galaxy, no."

Omaron felt his mind spin. This was too much. "From another *GALAXY?*"

"The next one to this. One that will one day collide with yours in another few hundred million years."

"And you can cross galactic distances?"

The alien made a movement with its head and shoulders that Omaron decided was a shrug.

"Wormholes cross the galaxy in seconds. It's only a matter of degree."

Omaron was struggling to control his breathing. He was beginning to see opportunities...

"Is this your normal appearance?" Omaron thought he knew the answer.

In reply, the entity pulled off the material covering its face. Omaron studied the large eyes that were almost human, lipless mouth and pale skin. All of these could pass for human but for the nose. There was nothing there but two small holes. Apart from the unusual height and strange style of walking, it would not take a great deal to make these people pass as human.

"And how long have you been in our Galaxy?"

"Some fifty of your Yshan years, watching you and studying your history."

"What possible things can you find here that are not available in your own galaxy."

"Nothing really. But the planets of our galaxy are worn, tired, much harder to exploit. We need heavy metals, other minerals, food supplies. It is much easier to take it from here and you have far more than you need."

It was certainly a fact, Omaron knew, that the Yshan Empire had more planets teeming with minerals, agricultural surpluses and everything else than the Empire could possibly use. Many such planets had never even been touched.

"So why don't you just come and take it? We'd probably not even notice."

"The risk is too great. Your Imperial Fleet is immensely powerful and we could not sustain a war."

"Then why not approach us? Why not negotiate a trade in peace?"

"Our study of your Empire makes us believe that no holder of the Yshan Throne would ever accept an alien Empire taking your resources. And we have nothing to trade with for your wealth that you do not already have."

Omaron saw the answer but asked the question anyway, to be certain.

"And in return for such an arrangement, you will put me on the Galactic Throne?"

"We know who and what you are, Omaron Yshan."

"And just how would you get over the issue of the Star which has guided us for millennia? The people would never tolerate a change of Emperor without the Star's agreement."

The alien then gave Omaron the biggest shock of the whole astounding discussion.

"We also have a Star," it said.

Chapter 23

Henry sat in consultation with his favourite advisors in his private quarters. Kyle and Charlie sat holding hands on the settee next to his armchair. Josh had another armchair across from him and Captain Sestucal, once his school teacher, Ms Hickey took the third armchair. Coffee sat in a large urn on the coffee table between them and they all filled their mugs. All formality was forgotten in these sessions.

"You really should be involving the Imperial Committee, Henry," said the Captain.

"I trust this group more than anyone to tell me what's the best thing to do," said Henry. "Once you've done that, then I call on the Committee!"

"Hah!" Kyle snorted in amusement. "But I've got to say it, Henry, you grew up enormously in that meeting with your parents. You were absolutely in command, very regal."

"Too right," said Josh. "I had difficulties remembering little Henry who used to tag along with Charlie and me and played the meanest game of chess in the world!"

"It's hard to recall those days," said Henry. "Being a Galactic Emperor is a real buzz, I must say, but sometimes I think things were a lot simpler, then."

"It's called growing up, Henry," said the Captain. "The Star chose you."

"It sure was a great adventure back then," said Charlie. "I'll never forget the moment when you just pushed forward and held up the Star."

Henry chuckled. "My favourite memory is when Josh and Kyle and I and Miss Hickey were being attacked by Omaron and Sophie and you rode up on that enormous great horse of yours and rode them all down!"

For a while longer, the group discussed the events of that time fifteen years ago and then the Captain returned them to the present.

"There's no record of the Star ever doing anything like that," she said. "The worst that's ever happened is when it has told an Emperor to resign because he's lost the energy, or the health to keep going."

"I wonder if that's what it was all about," said Charlie, thoughtfully. "While my dear husband here has been at the Academy and flitting all over the Universe, I've been reading some materials of our history and I found some stuff that was never publicised during old Garamax's time."

"Such as?" asked Henry with interest.

"Do you know anything about the planet called Hinores?" replied Charlie.

Kyle looked interested. "I do. About thirty years ago, I think. A small industrial planet in the outer regions. Some form of famine broke out, if I remember right."

"That's the one," said Charlotte. "Trouble is, Garamax withheld the news and refused to supply food to it. Thousands died until word got out to a nearby system that provided the food. Garamax was furious apparently and suppressed the Council and their advice."

"Wow!" exclaimed Josh. "That doesn't sound like an Yshan King."

"It doesn't," agreed Charlie. "Trouble is, there are a couple of other nasties. Something went wrong with Garamax, maybe a mental problem, couldn't stand up to being Emperor. Then maybe the Star told him to resign and he refused."

"I wonder if that's it," said Kyle. "My father has said a couple of times once I'd grown up that maybe it was better that the Emperor was killed in that accident rather than be removed by the Star. He never said why."

"So what?" said Charlie. "You think he arranged with Omaron to feign his death and steal the Star during its dormant period, then he could return a few days later, miraculously saved and resume the throne and nobody would know?"

"I think that's it," said the Captain. "That's the only thing that could tie all these insane events together."

"But that means Omaron knew the aliens, he must have had contact with them in order to arrange this!" said Kyle.

"And then betrayed his brother by dumping him on that rotten little planet," added Josh, the horror showing on his face. "How could anyone do that?"

Henry pressed the communications button by his chair.

"Yes, Sire," said the voice of his private secretary immediately.

"Alden, arrange an autopsy on my father at once. Tell the pathologist to look carefully for any sign of brain damage or decay that could cause any change in behaviour."

"At once, Sire," said the young man and the connection was broken.

"Henry, you've had rotten luck with parents," said Josh. "Your foster parents on Earth were seriously unpleasant, and now this. How do feel about it all?

"Well, I never knew my real parents, after all," Henry replied. "So I can't relate to those two sour old people we just met and I can't feel anything about my father's death. I suppose I just wish I could have had real parents, but Kyle's mum and dad have been wonderful to me and I think of them as my family. Karocarl especially has been great as mentor and advisor. After all, no Emperor before me has ever had an ex-Emperor as a mentor. My mother has gone somewhere, she hates me, thinks I ordered the Star to kill her husband, so I doubt we'll have any further contact. I can't say I care much."

The Captain broke the small sadness in the room. "What have you decided about the aliens?" she asked.

"All of them are being sent back," said Henry. "Except for the Captain of the Flag Ship. All their ships have been disarmed, we've taken the cloaking mechanisms to see if there's anything we don't already know and Charlie's dad is having the time of his life with that! And there's something else. Captain Sestucal?"

"Yes, Sire?" The Captain's tone was formal again, recognising a pending order.

"I need you to keep your ship in orbit round Yshan as protection in case of other alien forces. Re-equip with Greg's amazing new torpedoes and be prepared for anything."

"Yes, Sire."

"And with your consent, I would like to assign Lieutenant Bradshaw to a critical mission."

Josh sat up straight. This was going to be more than critical, he knew.

"No problems, Sire," the Captain said. "If we're staying in orbit, my Navigation Officer has little to do."

"Thank you," said Henry. "Josh, we took the alien flagship's navigation computers. Somewhere in there must be the secret of intergalactic wormhole travel. Find it. Use my name to call on all the technical and mathematical help you need, but find the answer. One day, we're going to travel between galaxies and this little task will bring that day a lot closer."

"I'll find it," said Josh, exhilaration bubbling through his body like a spring flood.

"I have every faith in you, Josh!" said Henry with his old grin back. "And now we've sent the rest of the aliens home except for their Flagship, we'll interrogate their Commanding Officer and as we've got the language sorted, that'll be a lot easier. Then we'll have to focus on Omaron's role in all this."

"And Sophie's," added Kyle sadly.

"Yes," said Henry. "Sophie, too."

Chapter 24 – The Interrogation of Omaron

"This is a case of High Treason," said the Judge, Fleet Admiral Dumar Domas. "Consequently, Captain Sestucal, you cannot be on the Judging Panel at your rank, as well as because you have been involved with the accused on several occasions in which you displayed the highest standards of the Service. You may however, be called as a witness and you may ask Prosecuting Council to ask questions of the accused."

"Thank you, sir, I understand," replied the Captain and sat down.

"The others present with you, Lieutenants Yshan and Bradshaw and The Duchess of Moidari, the former Miss Charlotte Foster may also be called as witnesses to the events on Earth."

"Further," continued the Judge, "because of the nature of the case, we believe civil unrest could occur if details of the accused's actions and those of Emperor Garamax the Eighteenth were to be made public, I order that these proceedings be in private, under strict security. However, for the sake of accurate history for future citizens, the records will be released in one hundred years, or earlier if ordered by the Emperor."

The Admiral looked sternly round the almost empty courtroom. Seated alone in the witness box, Omaron looked small and frail. He was thin, his face lined, seemingly much older than his years. Only Charlie, Kyle and Josh sat with the Captain together with Henry's private secretary. Apart from the three judges, all Admirals, the prosecutor, an extraordinarily young-looking woman and the defence counsel, an elderly man with thick white hair, their two assistants and the Judge's secretary, the room was empty. The doors had been sealed.

"The accused will rise," said the Judge's secretary. Looking frightened, Omaron rose to his feet.

"Madam Prosecutor?" said the Judge and the young woman stood up.

"I am Commander Olian Rambert of the Imperial Fleet," she said. "Mr Yshan, I understand that you have agreed to give the full details of your actions in relation to this matter?"

Omaron tried to speak, gasped and then croaked, "Yes."

"The events from the time Emperor Garamax the Eighteenth approached you to feign his death and steal the Star in its dormant phase have been written out and shown to you and you accept them as accurate?"

"Yes," replied Omaron, more strongly this time.

"You have also signed a statement in which you describe the first meeting with the alien species, the deal you arranged and how you carried it out, especially the way in which you dropped the Emperor and his wife on a remote planet. Is that an accurate description of the events?"

"Yes," said Omaron again. He seemed like a man utterly without hope, his shoulders slumped, his face ashen.

"Then it simply remains for you to tell us how you involved Princess Sophie and what part she played in this appalling story. Are you willing to tell us all the details? We will of course be interrogating the Princess separately to validate this story."

"I am," said Omaron, still without any life in him.

"Why did you approach the Princess in the first place?" asked the Prosecutor.

"The Star told me to," said Omaron.

"The Star?" gasped the young woman.

For the first time, Omaron showed some vitality. He grinned without humour.

"Not our Star," he said. "Their Star."

* * *

Thirty-two years earlier

"You understand what we want of you?" asked the alien admiral.

"I do, but I can't work out the logistics," said Omaron. "Why have I not met your Emperor?"

"You won't," replied the alien. "Now, what do you need?"

"I can't work out how to mock up my brother's death and get him away from the scene without somebody seeing it."

"Why bother?" asked the admiral. "Why not just kill him in his room? Why rescue him?"

"Because the Star will know. I'll be arrested within minutes. And much as I hate him, he's still my brother. I want him removed, not dead. I can't commit murder."

"You're a weakling," sneered the alien. "But we will arrange it. Persuade him to observe the upcoming fleet war games from your flagship battle cruiser. A cloaked ship of our fleet will release one of your own torpedoes at your Emperor's ship and destroy it. But he will get advance warning of the precise time and he must take a life pod before the ship is hit. Another cloaked ship will pick him up. What do you want to do next?"

"Take him somewhere too far away for him ever to get back. Drop him in the life pod without his ever seeing you or your ship, somewhere where he and his wife can live. But he must not know of your existence for this plan to work."

"Agreed," said the alien officer. "Now you must meet somebody."

"Who?" asked Omaron, but the alien didn't reply, instead standing up and walking out of the room with a gesture for him to follow. Feeling less and less an equal partner in this conspiracy and more of a mere tool, Omaron followed a few steps down the corridor and stopped before a huge, steel door.

"In," said the officer and opened the door. Nervously, Omaron slowly walked in and found himself in a high, arched chamber with nothing in it but a white stone block in the centre.

On the block was another Star.

Stunned, Omaron took a step backward then steeled himself to walk toward the stone block and look at the crystal form lying there. It looked much like the Star of the Yshan Kings, but it had a dark blue tone to it. Struggling for breath, he stood motionless, not knowing what to do.

And then....

"Omaron Yshan, third son of the last Emperor, youngest brother of the current Emperor Garamax the Eighteenth, we welcome you to our service," said a soft, silent voice in his head.

Omaron gasped in shock. He had heard that the Yshan Star sometimes spoke to an Emperor, but rarely, providing advice and guidance only through ideas that the Emperor would believe to be his own, even if knowing the real source. He had never heard the voice of a Star himself.

"What is it you want of me?" he stammered.

"Only to give you advice," replied the silent voice in his head. "You will get all the help you need from my people, but I must tell you that you have a natural ally in somebody close to the throne."

"Who?" gasped Omaron, feeling overwhelmed with the events.

"Your niece, Sophie," replied the Star.

"But she's barely weeks old!" exclaimed Omaron. "How can you know what she is?"

"We know. Trust us. That child will be your best ally. When she is old enough, talk to her and you will see the truth. She will want the throne for herself and will do anything to get it. Recruit her. Use her for as long as she is useful. When you think the time is right, bring her to us, we will convince her that the throne is hers if she follows your guidance."

Omaron felt sweat breaking out all over his body and left the Chamber of the Dark Star.

* * *

The present

"And when did you first broach this subject with Princess Sophie?" asked the Prosecutor.

"When she was eight."

"And what response did you get?"

"Let's say I was astonished by her enthusiasm..."

Thirty-two years earlier

The girl has a mean look about her, thought Omaron, watching his brother's twins playing in the garden with some of the other palace children. He decided that it was interesting to see how she treated the children of servants, with arrogance and condescension, whereas Kyle treated everybody as a friend. He watched Sophie deliberately trip other children as they ran past her and snubbed those she considered beneath her. She was not popular with the other children who tended to avoid her and congregated round Kyle whenever possible.

It's time we talked, he decided and waited until he could get her alone. That time occurred two days later after the children had been out riding with several adults, himself included. He positioned himself next to her as they rubbed down their horses and slowed his pace so that he was almost the last to finish.

"Sophie, would you like to talk?" he asked as they walked away from the stables at the end of the line of riders.

"Of course, Uncle Omaron," she said with a glowing smile. Somehow, he suspected that she recognised a kindred soul in him.

"Let's go into the Rose Garden," he said. "It's very private."

A few minutes later, shielded from the palace windows by large rose bushes, they sat on a secluded bench.

"Tell me, Sophie," he began. "How is your father doing as Emperor?"

He was disturbed and yet pleased to see an expression of scorn cross her childish features.

"He's too soft," she replied. "He lets the people get away with *anything!* Did you see that newspaper report last week criticising him for spending too much on redecorating the palace reception rooms? He said nothing! I'd have had them arrested and in prison until they apologised!"

Ye gods, this child is eight! he thought. "And what about Kyle?"

"He's the same! Look at how he lets all those horrible kids play with him. They're *commoners!* They shouldn't even be allowed to play with royalty like us, they just don't know their places!"

More and more interesting, he thought. "So do you think you'd do a better job than either of them?"

"Of course, I would! For a start, I wouldn't let all those stupid people in the other planets get so much! They get everything they want."

"We're a very rich Empire," he said mildly.

"Only because we on Yshan made it so," she replied. "It's ours! We should keep it!"

Now's the time, he decided. *This will either make it all possible or have me arrested.*

"I think I know how we could make you the next Empress," he said.

"How!" Her eyes widened with excitement. "Uncle Omaron, tell me how! Please!"

"You really want that?"

"More than anything else! I know I'd be the greatest ruler in all our history!"

"Sophie, there's something I have to tell you. This is the greatest secret in the world and if you can keep it, I'll make sure you'll be the next Empress of the Galaxy and when you're still young."

"What, Uncle Omaron? Please tell me, I promise, I really promise I'll keep it."

And so it starts, he thought. *The Dark Star had better be right about this strange child or I'll be on a prison planet within days.* "It's about your Uncle Garamax," he began. "Now you know that he died in a battle cruiser explosion..."

The present

"And she kept her promise, obviously," said the prosecutor.

"She was no ordinary child. I think she is genuinely evil. She wanted her father dead, she wanted her twin brother dead, or if not dead, out of the way."

"And she was fully aware that you had dropped her Uncle, the Emperor on a bleak planet thousands of light years from Yshan, stolen the Star and kidnapped the Prince Garamax who was two years old?"

"She knew all that and strongly approved."

The Judge stirred from his silent attention to the story.

"Defence Counsel, is there anything you want to say?"

The middle-aged man rose to his feet. "Your Honour, there is little I can do. Against all my advice, the defendant chose to give the entire details of his own free will. I can challenge nothing in the Prosecutor's case."

The judge nodded.

"Continue, Madam Prosecutor."

"So when did you introduce Princess Sophie to the Alien race?" asked the Prosecutor.

"During her exile on a remote planet."

"And you fully explained the details of the arrangement you had made?"

"Not quite. I told her the deal included her as Empress, not me as Emperor."

"She approved?"

"Enthusiastically."

"So can it be said, Mr Yshan, that both of were thoroughly involved in a plot to allow an alien invasion of the Empire and the replacement of the Star-appointed Emperor with one of yourselves in return for free exploitation of a number of planets within the Empire, many of which might have been occupied by citizens of the Empire?"

"Yes," said Omaron, his face staring at his feet. "It can be said."

"The Prosecution rests its case, Your Honour."

Chapter 25

Sub-Lieutenant Josh Bradshaw, newly-commissioned officer in the Imperial Fleet was having the time of his life. Sitting in the computer centre of the Fleet Academy, he was surrounded by monitors attached to the Academy's computers and the navigation system taken from the flag ship of the defeated alien fleet. Available to him was a group of some of the best technical geniuses, mathematicians, astrophysicists and language experts in the Galaxy.

After three weeks of probing, testing, analysing and a mixture of failures and successes, Josh felt they were nearly there.

The mathematicians had devised an interpreter that restructured the alien mathematics into their own forms. The astrophysicists had examined the records of the ship's flight and with the help of the reformatted mathematics, traced the origins of the fleet back to a planet in the nearest Galaxy, one that Charlie's father said was known on Earth as the Greater Magellanic Cloud.

Josh was deep into the last task, analysing the wormhole characteristics that had brought the massive fleet across inter-Galactic space in a matter of hours. He had barely slept the last three weeks, often forgetting to eat, not realising that food had been left by his side and removed, untouched some hours later.

He was getting close, he knew it. His extraordinary sense of wormhole structure and how to use it had startled even Greg, Charlie's father, a genius in his own right who had designed the torpedos that had disabled the invaders and was now leading a science department at the Yshan Imperial University.

The two were now looking at the columns of data spewed out by the alien navigation system and comparing them to the conversion tables produced by the University mathematicians.

"That can't work," said Josh in irritation. "They can't go in at that angle, that would bring them out within their own galaxy. Unless the speed... hand me that printout, will you Greg?"

For a few moments, the two men studied the figures before Greg suddenly let out a shout.

"Hey! That conversion of that alien symbol is wrong! Look! If you put the correct digit in, that changes everything!"

Josh sat down on his chair, almost weak with shock.

"I've got it," he said. "Now I can see how we can cross intergalactic space."

* * *

"It's all much the same as what we've been doing before," he said to the assembled group of scientists in the conference room of the University. It had been nearly two days since his shocking discovery of an error in the conversions that had hidden the truth from him, but now he stood confidently addressing some of the most extraordinary minds in the Yshan Empire.

"It's all in the different angles, entry speeds and entry points that gives us the intergalactic transitions," Josh continued. "What the aliens discovered is that if you enter the wormhole at a minimum of point nine nine eight Light and at far more extreme angles and almost right on the edge, a whole different set of effects occurs."

A hand shot up from the back row of the auditorium.

"Have you tested this?" asked a tall, balding man that Josh knew was the head of Quantum Chemistry at the University.

Charlie's father took up the story.

"We equipped a dozen torpedoes with quantum radio so that we got instantaneous communication at any distance. We fired them through the local wormhole at different speeds, angles and entry points, but all within the limits that Josh has discovered and then recorded their arrivals. I have to tell you, the results were startling! Three of them arrived within minutes in the Greater Magellanic, the galaxy containing the alien home world, four went to a further galaxy some fifteen million light years away and the remaining five went in one jump to the very far end of our own galaxy."

There was a brief whisper of amazement from the group.

"We've taken all the figures," continued Greg, "and developed complete navigation charts for at least the two nearest galaxies to us. Our ships can go just about anywhere we want."

This time, the applause from the group was long and loud.

Chapter 26

"Emperor Garamax, we must talk."

The voice sounded persistently in Henry's dreams until slowly he woke up.

It was the Star! After several years of his reign, this was the first time the Star had communicated with him directly. While he knew that several decisions he had made had been somehow guided by the Star, it had never spoken directly to him. For a moment, he felt irritation.

"Did you really have to wake me up?" he said. "Couldn't this have waited till daytime?"

"An Emperor is always surrounded by people during the day," replied the soft voice in his head. "And the noise can crowd out our communication."

"I see," said Henry, tension rising as he realised the Star would never talk to the Emperor unless something serious was threatening. "Do you wish me to come to the Chamber?"

"No need," said the Star. "Here is where you are comfortable."

Henry waited, no lessening of the tension. He got out of the bed and sat down in the armchair by the window.

"Henry, great dangers threaten the Empire," said the Star.

"Henry? You call me Henry? Why is this?"

"Perhaps it's a sign to what we have to tell you. We know that have never been comfortable with your legal name and that you take great comfort in the company of the friends of those childhood days."

"This is true. But what are the dangers threatening us?"

"Great forces are gathering against the Empire. And we are not certain that we can defend against them as our own time is coming to an end."

"The Star is dying?" gasped Henry in massive shock.

"In a sense. But the great danger is against the Empire, whether a Star is there or not. The forces you defeated will return and they have allies."

"The aliens? We disarmed them so thoroughly, I can't see how they can restore their power for many years."

"They have resources, Henry. Far worse, they have assistance like myself as well as allies here."

"There is another Star?" Henry was shaken.

"Why should you doubt it?" asked the soft voice. "There is no reason that we should be the only one of our kind."

For a moment, Henry was more fascinated by that fact than the dangers of which the Star had warned him. Then he forced his mind back to the problem.

"What must I do?" he asked.

"You must go away," said the Star. "You must seek out the forces that will help you."

"But where?" asked Henry in desperation. "Where in all the Galaxy can I look for such help?"

"Remember your origins, Henry."

For a moment, Henry thought the Star had slightly emphasised his name as if hinting at something.

"Remember also the origins of the Yshan Empire, how your people were saved from oblivion. This is where you will find help again."

"And how long have we got while you are still with us?" asked Henry, feeling a huge sense of loss that soon the Star might end its time with the Yshan people.

But there was no reply.

* * *

For two days, Henry stayed private. He assigned authority for decisions to the Imperial Council and sat alone in deep thought. Finally he used his private communications system and called the battle cruiser in orbit around the planet.

"Captain Sestucal, please hand over command to your First Officer with the rank of Acting Captain."

"Yes, Sire," she said formally, revealing no reaction.

"Then you and Lieutenants Bradshaw and Kyle report to me at the palace as soon as you can. Be prepared to be away for a considerable time."

Again, she revealed nothing, but acknowledged the order and ended the communication.

Henry pressed another button.

"Charlie, I need you here," he said.

"Be there in five minutes," said Charlie.

Henry sat back to wait for the people he trusted more than anyone in the Galaxy to come and join him.

* * *

"I have to go away," Henry said with little warning

when they were all seated in his private quarters.

A small sigh ran round the room but nobody displayed any greater shock than that.

Henry quickly gave them a summary of what the Star had told him.

"How do you interpret what it said?" asked Kyle. "That bit about your origins and the stuff about the beginnings of the Yshan Empire, do you understand it?"

"I do," said Henry. He looked round the room. Brad and Josh looked badly shaken by the developments, Charlie was almost in tears. Only Captain Sestucal looked unmoved, sitting calmly with a trace of a smile on her face.

"You understand, don't you, Ms Hickey?" said Henry with a wide grin.

"Yes, Henry, I do," she replied. "We go to Earth, all of us, the old gang. And somehow we have to find the First."

It took some time for the excitement to die down before they could resume the serious discussion.

"You have to appoint a Regent in your place, Henry," said Kyle. "Any ideas?"

"Pretty obvious Kyle, your dad!" replied Henry. "After all, he's had more experience as Emperor than I have and he was a really good one, too."

"Perfect!" said Josh.

"And what about Sophie and Omaron?" asked Kyle.

"Omaron is exiled for life, never to come within two hundred light years of Yshan," Henry said. "He's been fitted with an ankle chain that cannot be removed and that will warn the prison authorities if he approaches within his limits. He knows it will mean life in prison if that happens. He has forfeited all his possessions, all titles. His Star

Medallion had long since gone dead, but that's been taken from him, anyway. I think he'll die in poverty."

"And I have no sympathy with him at all," said Kyle. "I never could stand the man, even when I was a kid. And my sister?"

"The prosecutor argued for the same penalty," said Henry sadly. "But I overruled her. Sophie may stay on Yshan, but like Omaron, she will be stripped of all possessions, title and Star Medallion. She has until the end of the week to vacate the Palace."

Kyle wiped a tear from one eye. "Honestly, Henry, you've been too lenient. I know she's my twin sister, but she really is a truly evil person."

"I think so, too," said Henry. "Luckily, there's not much else she can do to hurt the Empire."

"I hope so," said Charlie. "When do we set off?"

"In a week," replied Henry. "I have a lot to before I can quit the throne."

Chapter 27

Charlie had found it hard to sleep since the enormous news had been delivered of Henry's coming quest to Earth to find the mythological race of beings known throughout Yshan history as "The First."

She and Kyle had an enormous amount of work to do in order to prepare, not least of which was saying goodbye to her parents. She had closed down their house, stored their furniture and belongings in a secure location and assigned the administrative functions that she had as a member of the Yshan Royal Family to trusted agents. But with two days to go before their planned departure in Henry's personal cruiser, she found herself restless, unable to sleep at all.

She stared at the clock by her bed. Kyle was deeply asleep and she envied him that ability. Deciding that remaining there was pointless, she got up and dressed in jeans and tee-shirt, thinking that a walk in the gentle warm air of the Palace gardens might help her settle her mind.

She left the private suite that was their residence while waiting to leave for Earth and made her way along the corridors. As she passed the short corridor leading to the Emperor's private suite, she stopped in surprise.

"Sophie!" she exclaimed.

The astonished look of appalling guilt told Charlie everything.

"You've been into Henry's room!" she said. "What have you done?"

Recovering her composure, Sophie smirked.

"Whatever it is, silly little Earth girl, there's nothing you can do about it!"

"Sophie, you're insane," snapped Charlie. "You must know there are cameras guarding the entire building. You've been spotted already!"

"Do you think I could have lived half my life here without knowing how the security systems work and how to turn them off?" said Sophie with a laugh.

"But now I know," said Charlie. "But I need to see how the Emperor is and if you've harmed him..."

"You'll do what?" said Sophie with a cold smile. "You think you can get past me?"

"Maybe," replied Charlie.

Sophie's smile broadened into a wide grin.

"Let's see then, shall we?" she said and took two paces towards Charlie and drove a hard fist straight at Charlie's head.

Charlie merely leaned sideways a few degrees and the shot missed her by a centimetre. She flicked her right hand up, seized hold of Sophie's wrist and jerked Sophie round violently, throwing her against the wall.

Sophie's eyes widened in shock, but she flung herself at Charlie, spun and aimed a head high kick. Charlie ducked with incredible speed, the flying kick went above her head and Charlie moved forward far enough to land a vicious punch in Sophie's middle and as the taller girl bent double in pain, Charlie raised her knee into Sophie's face and smashed her nose into jelly.

Sophie collapsed, barely conscious. She stared up at Charlie in rage and fear. "How...?" she gasped, wiping blood from her nose.

Charlie bent over and pulled Sophie's Star Medallion from under her shirt. There was no gleam of light in the middle. Then she pulled a similar Medallion out from under her own shirt. The gleam of the Star shard lit up the gloomy corridor.

"You think I've just been sitting around all day since I came here?" she said. "I've had lots of time to learn things and Kyle reckons I'm as good as he is now. And the Star decided I should have its protection."

She stood back as doors were flung open and armed guards raced in.

"Look after her," snapped Charlie and ran into Henry's room. He was lying on his back, seemingly asleep, but there was not even the suspicion of breathing in his chest.

"Doctors!" screamed Charlie. "Get doctors in here! The Emperor is ill!"

Then she collapsed weeping at Henry's side.

*　*　*

"I don't think there are any ill effects," said Henry sitting in his favourite armchair.

For two days he had been held in hospital while a team of doctors and specialists in various drugs and medicines poured over him, took samples and fed him a cocktail of complex compounds and mixtures. Finally, they pronounced him healthy but were baffled by what Sophie had injected into him.

"But there's no doubt you'd have been dead in a few more minutes if we hadn't got to you," said the chief surgeon. "But whatever that was in your system, it seems to have vanished without trace."

"They say you're fit to travel," said Kyle. "So are we leaving tomorrow as planned?"

Henry nodded. "You father is being sworn in as Emperor Regent today."

"And Sophie?" asked Charlie.

Henry grimaced. "No more favours, no concessions," he said. "The attempted murder of the Emperor gets nothing but a life sentence in prison. She won't see outside the walls of the maximum security jail again."

"It's impossible to believe that she and Kyle are twins," said Josh. "Such two opposite, it's quite irrational."

Henry stood up. "One more thing to do," he said. "All of you come with me, we need to pay a last visit to the Star."

The group stood up and followed him out of the room to the Chamber of the Star. Henry stopped by the door, smiled at his friends then opened it.

They filed in and stopped in incredible shock.

The Star's light had gone out.

Chapter 28

"It does feel so strange being back here," said Charlie.

"Doesn't look all that different, does it?" said Josh with a laugh. "Just one extra building by the library, that's it."

"And how do we start the search for the First?" asked Josh. "I could never have thought they'd be on Earth for a start and we have the whole planet!"

"My suggestion," said Captain Sestucal, "is that we have a look at that barn where we found the Star."

She looked a lot like the young Ms Hickey they had known as a teacher at this small school twelve years ago. She'd abandoned her Navy uniform in favour of ordinary jeans and sweater and an Akubra hat had replaced her officer's cap.

Henry nodded. "With no other ideas being any better, let's do it."

They had been on Earth for a week and found nothing. Josh and Kyle were very edgy, wishing they could return to active duty on the Battle Cruiser, Charlie was more concerned with Henry's health and Henry himself seemed listless and low on energy.

"I'm really worried about this," Charlie said to Ms Hickey as they walked back to the big station wagon they had hired for their stay. Surprisingly, the Captain had produced an apparently valid driving licence and a legal address in Sydney when renting the car, but nobody had wanted to raise the issue with her.

"Why's that?" replied Ms Hickey.

"Why would the First be here on Earth?" said Charlie. "It makes no sense. And what happens if we find them? Why would they want us to find them, anyway?"

"Good questions," replied Ms Hickey. "But the Star did tell Henry to bring us all here, I assume it had good reasons."

Charlie looked doubtful. "Maybe. But I wonder if those reasons were for Henry's sake or its own?"

"What a curious thing to say!" Ms Hickey looked hard at Charlie. "What do you really mean?"

Charlie looked distressed. "I don't know," she whispered. "But something's wrong, I'm sure of it. Anyway, I think we should get Henry back into hospital, he's clearly not well."

Ms Hickey didn't reply as she climbed into the driver's seat and waited for the others to take their seats, Charlie threw a few glances at her as they drove off, but the woman's face remained expressionless. Charlie said nothing more.

The old barn didn't seem to have changed in the decade or more since they had discovered the Star in its basement. There was no lock on the door and they walked in to see much as they had seen all those years ago, a bare floor with a thin layer of straw on it.

"I think the trap door was.... here," said Kyle and reached down, shifted a small handful of straw and opened the handle that was revealed.

A step ladder was in place. Ms Hickey took a tiny illuminating lamp from her pocket and climbed down first and as the rest followed, the room was brightly lit.

"Wow!" said Josh. "Remember the last time we were here? When Henry first held up the Star!"

For a moment, they were all lost in the extraordinary memories of that event.

"But there's nothing here," said Charlie, her voice breaking as she held back the tears. "This has all been a waste of time! Please, let's get back home, Henry should be in Hospital."

There was a tiny buzz and Ms Hickey took out a tiny communicator. She listened for a second.

"Yes," she said. "We need to get back to the Ship. Something has happened."

"What is it?" demanded Josh as they returned to the car.

"I don't know yet," replied Ms Hickey. "That was a call from the Admiral. He needs to talk to us."

The hour long drive back to the woodland where they had landed the small cruiser was passed in silence. Quickly, they climbed out and walked into the ship.

"Take us up, Kyle!" ordered the Captain and without any motion being detected, the visual screens showed the Earth far below them and vanishing within minutes.

The screen on one wall switched views and the face of the Fleet Admiral appeared.

"Your Majesty," said the Admiral. "Captain, and the others with you. I have to tell you that the alien fleet reappeared in Yshan space a few hours ago. Somehow, they had replenished their weapons and they destroyed the three ships that we had in our region. Your cruiser, captain, managed to escape. All our other ships were in distant regions. I gave them orders to implement Code Ninety and they have, so they should be safe."

"Code Ninety?" murmured Kyle.

"Wait!" snapped the Captain.

"Tragically," continued the Admiral, "the enemy destroyed our Fleet Headquarters and with it, almost all our senior officers. I was returning from a meeting and somehow survived, but I will not be able to get away and I believe my ship will be hunted down and destroyed within hours or less. I therefore order you, Captain, to implement Code Ninety as well. When you meet up with the remaining fleet, you will assume the rank of Admiral and take command of the fleet until such time as a response can be arranged."

"Yes sir," replied the Captain, showing no emotion.

"There is worse," continued the Admiral. "Alien forces have taken over the city, the Palace and all government buildings. There is little left of our military forces and I have to advise that Princess Sophie has been freed from her prison and has declared herself Empress. We cannot access the Star and with the alien power behind her, there is little we can do."

"Is there much damage to the city, Admiral?" asked Henry.

"Very little, Your Majesty, but the Palace is totally destroyed. We can't be certain, but we have little hope of finding the Emperor Regent and his wife alive."

Kyle let out a small sob then forced self control on himself.

"I'm so sorry, Kyle," said the Admiral. "Captain, God Speed and I can only hope..."

The screen faded and went black.

The Captain turned away, her mouth a tight, grim line.

"Code Ninety," she said. "After Josh had developed the methodology and navigation techniques for inter-galactic travel, every ship of the fleet, including this one was equipped with automatic navigation systems to cross to a galaxy quite remote from the Yshan Empire. It was considered possible that we would see exactly what has just happened. Josh, take the Navigation console please."

She was the Navy Captain again. Josh automatically followed her order and went to the large screen.

"Enter the following digits, Josh," the Captain said and recited a series of codes which Josh carefully entered on his keypad.

"Done, Ma'am," he said.

"Now, take us to Wormhole AQJ91D," she ordered. "When in range, the computer will take over and pilot us the rest of the way."

"We're crossing inter-galactic space, Captain?" asked Henry.

"We are, Sire," she replied. "It will take us just three hours after entering the wormhole."

"Good grief," murmured Henry and collapsed on the floor.

Charlie let out a cry and rushed to him. Kyle went to the medical cabinet and brought out a variety of instruments and brought them to her, but after only a few seconds, she sat up, tears flowing down her face.

"It must have been what Sophie injected in him," she sobbed. "The doctors thought they'd got it all out, but they didn't. Henry's dead. Emperor Garamax the Nineteenth is dead."

Chapter 29 - Finale

The ship met up with the four hundred or so remaining ships of the Yshan Imperial Fleet several hours later. The welcome was enormous as the fleet believed that Henry was with them, but the Captain broadcast the news, followed by the replay of the Admiral's last message.

Every Captain in the fleet signalled their acknowledgement of the Captain's new position as the Commanding Officer of the Fleet.

"First orders," she said. "Spread out, find a suitable planet for us to take over as our new home and report back as you find them. Everybody stay in touch and one day we'll correct this horrible development and rebuild the Yshan Empire."

She turned back to the others.

"I think perhaps that's why the Star sent us on this quest. Not to find the First, but just to get Henry out of the way of what it knew was happening."

"I think the Empire is going to have dreadful times while Sophie rules it with the help of the aliens," said Kyle. He had his arm round Charlie who was still shaking with grief.

"Then it's up to us to do something," said Josh. "However long it takes."

"But first we have to find a home planet," said the Captain.

"When we do, I think we'll call it Henry," said Josh, smiling for the first time since they'd landed on Earth.

Everybody agreed.

Part Three

The Star of the New Yshan Empire

Chapter 30

Commander Kyle Yshan knew he was in the battle of his life.

The alien battle cruiser was firing torpedo after torpedo at Kyle's frigate and the frigate's pilot was somehow avoiding each one with a demonstration of extraordinary flying skills.

"They're tracking us!" exclaimed the First Officer. She seemed calm, but Kyle knew she was almost certainly feeling the same high tension that he was experiencing. "Somehow they can track us while we're cloaked!"

"Navigator, how far to the wormhole?" snapped Kyle.

"Eight minutes, fifteen seconds, NOW!" replied the Lieutenant at the Nav Console.

"Guns, are the torpedoes armed?"

"Armed and ready," replied the officer at the gunnery control.

"Fire one and two," ordered Kyle. There was no sensation, but the rear screen showed two tiny sparks flying back to the invisible shape of the alien cruiser. They glowed briefly.

"Anything?" asked Kyle.

"They're still following," reported the First Officer. "They must have learned how to counteract them."

"Charlie's dad wouldn't like to hear that," said Kyle calmly, although inside he felt dismay and some fear. The torpedoes had been the critical weapon in defeating the alien fleet when it first attacked the Yshan Empire over a century ago. They had been designed by one of the most famous scientists in Yshan history, the father of Charlotte Foster, the bride of the first Kyle Yshan. Charlie was still a revered historical figure, and Kyle always revelled in the fact that she was his great, great grandmother and he had pulled many strings to get the command of this frigate, the *"Charlie Foster."*

The ship shuddered as a massive explosion occurred somewhere off the starboard side. Kyle grabbed his armrests and hung on, but several people on the bridge were knocked off their feet.

"Oooh, ever so close!" said the pilot, looking quite unconcerned.

"Report!" snapped Kyle into the ship's communications, but the only responses he got were a series of "No Damage" statements from the various locations.

"Six minutes to the wormhole," reported the Navigator. Only a slight hoarseness in his voice revealed the fear that all of them were feeling.

The frigate had been returning from a routine patrol of the borders of the old Yshan Empire, now controlled by the aliens. They had encountered the battle cruiser when they were just three light years from the old Yshan Home world but the first they knew about it was the alarm indicating an incoming missile. Only the extraordinary piloting skills of Lieutenant Bradshaw had let them dodge the missile and that was the only defence the frigate had now.

"Incoming," reported the First Officer as another missile approached.

"Got it!" snapped the pilot and calmly watched his screen as the torpedo approached, then at the last micro-second threw the frigate into a looping roll and they watched the missile flash past.

"Well done, Mr Bradshaw," said Kyle. "Nav?"

"Three minutes to wormhole."

"Sir, if they get this close, they'll be able to follow us through the wormhole," said the First Officer. Only the tightness in her hands as she clutched the arm rest of her seat betrayed the worry. "That would give away our location to the aliens."

"What a great idea, Number One," replied Kyle. "Bradshaw, can you keep us alive another three minutes."

"Yes sir!" said the pilot. "Keep watching this space!"

Kyle pressed the button on the quantum radio on his arm rest.

"Control, this is Commander Kyle Yshan. Do you read?"

The response was instantaneous. "Go ahead, Commander."

"We will enter the wormhole in two minutes. We are being pursued by a battle cruiser. It is fully cloaked but it will be just seconds behind us. Arrange a hot welcome, please. Use conventional torpedoes, the disabling systems no longer work."

"Noted, Commander," said the disembodied voice. "We're cooking up a storm for you."

Kyle grinned and disconnected the radio that used quantum physics to communicate across even intergalactic distances. Looking across at his First Officer, he saw by her own smile that she'd got the point of this manoeuvre.

For another two minutes, the deadly game continued and the pilot displayed almost magical reflexes and flying skills to avoid the torpedoes that kept coming from the invisible cruiser.

"Wormhole ahead!" reported the Navigation Officer. "Entry direction and impact speed calculated."

"Take us through, Lieutenant," ordered Kyle.

"Entering at Light 998," said the Navigation Officer.

The massive ring of fire that was the wormhole blazed into existence ahead and the crew barely had time to see the ring flash by. But instead of the expected sight of the stars of their home galaxy covering the entire field of vision, they found themselves in what seemed like a thick cloud of dust.

"Clever," said Kyle. "They've spread dust all over the place! The battle cruiser may be cloaked but the dust will reveal it. Pilot, turn ninety degrees to port, get us out of here!"

"Ninety to port, aye, sir!" replied Lieutenant Bradshaw and though nothing could be seen in the visual screens, the instruments showed the change of direction.

"Rear vision!" ordered Kyle. Just as he spoke, the screen cleared as they left the dust cloud that had been blown out by the Yshan fleet. They could now see the vast volume of space that was filled with dust and in the middle of it, the billowing clouds that revealed the transit of the enemy battle cruiser.

Massive explosions erupted around the cruiser as it was hit by conventional torpedoes. Its cloaking systems must have failed because the enormous sphere became visible and that gave the fleet fighters a chance to target it more accurately.

"They got the drives!" exclaimed the First Officer and a cheer rang out on the bridge as the cruiser became immobilised.

"Well done, everybody," said Kyle, at last breathing more easily. "Mr Bradshaw, where did you learn to fly like that?"

Lieutenant Bradshaw grinned cheerfully and switched on the automatic pilot, turning in his seat to face the Commander.

"Family archives, sir," he said. "I found out that the great grandfather of the first Josh Bradshaw had flown in what was called World War Two back on Earth. He flew a fighter aeroplane called a "Hurricane" and apparently he was a real ace! I've been able to find some film of that war when I took a trip back to Earth and I studied the flight techniques!"

"Just as well for us," said Kyle. "We should have you assigned to the Fleet Academy to teach the pilots."

The conversation was ended with a call from the First Officer.

"Fleet Admiral Bradshaw calling, sir!"

"Put him on," said Kyle and the large screen filled with the face of the Admiral, the Commander-in-Chief of the Yshan Fleet. Kyle knew the man was in his sixties but the face still exuded energy and a power of command that left nobody unaffected.

Kyle threw a smart salute. "Good morning, sir!"

"Well done, Commander," replied the Admiral. "And congratulations to your crew, they performed superbly. Though you took a bit of a risk."

Feeling the exhilaration of surviving a life-threatening battle and knowing how well the crew had performed, Kyle took a little more risk.

"Thank you, sir," he said. "But look what followed me home! Can we keep it?"

Around him, he heard the muffled laughter of his crew, also feeling the slightly unbalanced euphoria of surviving combat. The Admiral's lips twitched slightly.

"Will you promise to feed it properly and take it for walkies every day?"

The crew were struggling and Kyle knew they'd collapse into hysteria very soon.

"I promise, sir!" he said.

"Very good," the Admiral replied. "My office as soon as you can get here," and disconnected the call. But before the vision faded, Kyle was certain he heard the Admiral start a sustained belly laugh, but it was hidden behind the explosive hysteria of his own crew.

Chapter 31

The Fleet Admiral's office was spacious, with the commander's desk at one end and a conference table to seat twenty at the other. In between was a more casual area, a coffee table with four armchairs around it.

Kyle walked in as the door was opened by a young woman lieutenant who served as the Admiral's executive assistant. He threw a smart salute at the Admiral seated behind his desk. The older man stood up and smiled, pointing at the coffee table.

Around the walls was a series of portraits of every generation of the Bradshaw and Yshan families. Immediately behind the Admiral's desk was a set of five portraits. The first Kyle Yshan, Duke of the Moidari Sector, Guardian of the Six Home Planets and Prince of the Royal House of Yshan looked out at the room with a faint smile of pride, as if aware of his descendents. Next to him was the painting of his wife, Charlotte Foster, once of Australia, Planet Earth, always known as Charlie. Next to Charlie, the face was of a slight, fair-haired, handsome young man, the last

Yshan Emperor, Garamax 19th who had been poisoned by his cousin, Sophie, the twin sister of Kyle. Next was the first Josh Bradshaw. Like Charlie, he was originally of Australia, Planet Earth and he looked sternly out onto the room.

The final picture was of a tall, handsome woman in the uniform of the Fleet and the badges of rank of an Admiral. This was the legendary Kandria Sestucal, the first Admiral of the Imperial Fleet after it had fled to the new Galaxy. She had vanished just ten years after that event, leaving no traces of any kind or any clues as to what had happened.

These five had been the principal players in the drama that had ended with the defeat of the Yshan Empire by the alien forces that now controlled it and the flight of the remaining ships of the Yshan Imperial Fleet to a galaxy far distant from the one-time Empire. Each generation of both families had by tradition named the first-born sons and daughters with the name of the first of the line. The history of those adventures was firmly fixed in the legends of the Yshan Empire, including the story of how Emperor Garamax 19th had been found on Earth as a small boy called Henry, abandoned there by another of the Yshan line, Omaron, the Uncle of the first Kyle and his twin sister Sophie, both of them known as the greatest traitors in Yshan history. There were no portraits of either Sophie or Omaron on these walls.

Kyle was the fifth to bear the name of his ancestor.

Fleet Admiral Josh Bradshaw was the fourth of his line.

"Take a seat, Kyle," the Admiral said. "Would you arrange coffee, Samalin?" he added to the assistant. Without a word, she left.

Kyle removed his uniform cap, waited for the Admiral to sit down then took a seat across from him. The placing at the coffee table indicated an informal chat, rather than a formal discussion of military affairs.

"That was quite an action, Kyle," said the Admiral.

"I'm still breathing hard," replied Kyle. "But when my First Officer said they were close enough to follow us through the wormhole, I got the idea that capturing the ship would be a good idea."

"But did you think they might broadcast the details back to their headquarters and we might expect an invasion fleet at any time?"

Kyle sat still. He realised that he hadn't thought about that and felt chilled at the idea.

"No, sir," he said softly. "That was a mistake."

"But as it turned out, a risk worth taking," the Admiral said. "Our technicians have gone through the ship's computer records and it looks like they didn't pass the details of the wormhole entry back home, only the fact that they were in pursuit of an Yshan warship. As far as the aliens are concerned, their ship has just vanished. And the main development, a massive one, is that we know now that our disabling torpedoes no longer work on their ships. Can you imagine if we'd begun the invasion of our old territories armed with those torpedoes?"

"It would have been fatal for us," said Kyle. "But now we have an alien ship to examine and find something that can damage them."

"Exactly," said the Admiral and paused as the door opened and the young woman arrived, wheeling a trolley with a coffee pot and cups and all the trimmings. She poured two cups for the men at the table and left without a word.

Kyle drank his coffee black, but he waited while the Admiral added sweetener and cream to his.

"What will you do with the crew of that ship, sir?" Kyle asked.

An expression of distaste crossed the older man's face.

"I've no idea, to be honest," he replied. "The interrogators are tackling them of course, but I doubt there's anything else they can tell us that we don't already know. I'm afraid they're facing a long period of captivity. I can't say I have any sympathy for them."

Kyle sipped his coffee and changed the subject. "Your grandson did a magnificent job avoiding the torpedoes," he said. "Apparently he's been studying fighter techniques from an old Earth war."

The Admiral smiled proudly. "So he told me! It looks like we could adopt some of those ideas for all our pilots. I've told the Academy to set up an advanced flying section to teach them. Young Josh can go and be the first instructor."

"Sir, you mentioned the invasion. Is that really in planning now?"

The Admiral looked serious. "It's been in planning ever since we came here a hundred and twenty years ago. But our first priorities of course were to set up our own nation, develop industries, towns and explore the galaxy that we'd taken over. Now we have an empire of our own, with over sixty planets colonised and prosperous and I suppose we wouldn't be too serious about returning home under normal circumstances. But the spies we've had back there report that things are ugly, just as you have also reported. Whole worlds have been looted to serve the aliens, it's a real tyranny in charge and the people are desperate. Apparently the original Sophie became Empress and she's got some descendant, also called Sophie who's just as appalling as the first. Of course, you're related to her, Kyle, so you won't like to hear that."

Kyle stirred uncomfortably. "No, I really don't," he said. "It's always worried me that the Yshan family could produce somebody as evil as Sophie and her Uncle Omaron, while the rest of us seemed to be pretty good people. It's odd that she seems to have carried on the same tradition of naming her female descendents after herself. Do we know any more about the family?"

"Not a thing," replied old Josh Bradshaw. "It's peculiar, our spies should have found out something. We've got copies of their school books and encyclopaedias but there's no mention of the first Sophie ever having a family. But the present one is clearly running a terrible regime and our people are suffering as you saw yourself. An invasion is essential."

"But they have their Star," replied Josh. "Can we invade while they still have that?"

"It's the main question," agreed the Admiral. He looked down at the medallion hanging on his chest. It was a plain silver disk but in the centre was a tiny speck of light, too small for the particle emitting it to be measured. "You and I and my sister are the only people in the Galaxy to have these. We all pray that they indicate that some day, the Star of the Yshan Kings will be reborn and guide us as it once did. The fact that these specks stay alive gives us hope that it will happen."

Kyle touched the twin of the disk hanging round his own neck. There were only three of these, all that was left of the large crystal that had guided the Yshan family over five thousand years from a small, dying clan on a dying planet to the leadership of a Galactic Empire extending over several thousand worlds. Since fleeing the old empire, Yshan legends had grown that one day, a new star would be born, to replace the one that had died as the alien fleet had defeated the old

Empire. The medallions were passed down through the generations and Kyle had received his when his father had died just two years ago.

"However," the Admiral broke into the small silence. "It's clear that the aliens don't know where we are and thanks to you, we know that the weapon we would have depended on would not work. We have the alien ship and our people are tearing it apart to work out a new weapon. So yes, Kyle, we are planning an invasion, perhaps in two or three years."

That reminded Kyle that he'd forgotten one more surprise for the Admiral.

"With your permission, Sir?" he asked as he touched the communicator on his lapel.

The Admiral nodded, with a slightly puzzled expression.

"Bring him in," said Kyle and immediately, there was a knock on the door and it opened. Two large, armed men of the Fleet Military Police walked in with a much smaller man between them. They saluted the Admiral and left.

The newcomer was small, slightly built, looked about forty years old and badly frightened.

The Admiral stared at him, frowning.

"Kyle?" he said.

"With your permission, Sir," said Kyle. "May I present a man who calls himself Omaron Yshan."

The Admiral looked shaken. "You'd better explain," he said.

Chapter 32 – A Week Earlier

Kyle and his First Officer, Martina Corralon walked slowly along the sidewalk in the city that was still the capital of the Empire. Sometimes it amused Kyle that so many women had adopted the fashion of using Earth names, ever since his great, great grandmother, Charlotte, known as Charlie had been such a famous woman.

Once, this city had been the capital of the Yshan Empire, but over a century ago, the Aliens had invaded for the second time, destroying the small number of Yshan warships that had been near the Home Planet. The remainder of the fleet had fled, able to find a new Galaxy as a result of technology developed from alien ships captured during the first invasion and adapted by the genius of the first Josh Bradshaw.

The city had little resemblance to the city Kyle knew from his history books. Then, it had been rich, sophisticated and colourful, populated by a wealthy, peaceful civilisation that had grown up through a thousand years of the Galactic Empire, governed by the Yshan Family under the guidance of the Star of the Yshan Kings.

Now the place was dull, run-down, roads hadn't been maintained in decades, buildings were similarly decrepit and the people all looked miserable and poverty-stricken. It was a depressing sight. Kyle and his officer were dressed as locals in poorly-made clothing and they fitted in with the scene to give no cause for second looks.

The only traffic on the roads was military. Several times, open trucks had drifted through, floating a metre above the ground on anti-gravity engines that let them ignore the poor road surfaces, with half a dozen armed guards sitting with weapons ready for use. All the ones Kyle had seen so far were alien, very tall, elongated beings but mostly like humans other than their height and thin build. But one of the trucks was manned by Yshans, also in uniform and carrying weapons.

"Traitors," muttered a man next to Kyle and then looked terrified as Kyle turned to him.

"Relax, I'm with you," said Kyle. "So some people have joined the occupation army?"

"Where have you been all your life?" asked the man. "Lots of them have gone over to the Empress, may she die soon."

"It's our first time here," said Martina. "My brother and I have come up to see our mother, we live a long way south. Down there, we haven't seen any police but the aliens."

"Can we talk?" asked Kyle.

The man nodded and gestured for them to follow him. He led them down an alleyway between two ruined buildings and into what might once have been a pleasant square. Now it was filled with sad-looking people, cooking various meals over open fires. Even the children looked depressed and quiet.

The man led them to one section where a woman was boiling water over a fire made of household debris.

"My wife," he said. "Can we offer you tea?"

Realising how poor these people were, Kyle and Martina shook their heads but sat down on the ground.

"This is dreadful," said Kyle. "Is it the same everywhere?"

"As far as we know," replied the other woman. "The Demon Empress Sophie rules like a tyrant. She owns all the wealth and any disobedience is punishable by death. Most of the industry is dead except for mining and the aliens take all that back to their home world."

"Sophie?" asked Martina. "It can't be the original one, she'd be about a hundred and fifty years old."

"Dunno about that," muttered the man. "We don't get any schooling, so we only know a bit about history from stories passed down by a few people. But it can't be her, this one looks about twenty, very dark, very beautiful, very evil."

"So what do you know about our history?" asked Kyle.

"Not a lot. We know that aliens came one day and the Yshan Space Fleet vanished. The legend is that the Fleet went to another Galaxy and is building itself up again. All of us grow up dreaming of the day when the Fleet returns and destroys the Aliens, takes the Empress prisoner for trial and the Old Yshan Empire will be restored."

"It's a good dream," said Kyle. "Keep a firm grip on it for it will happen some day." He stood up, followed by Martina. "We must go," he said.

They walked back along the alley to the main street and as they emerged, another man stood before them. He looked about thirty, a few years younger than Kyle but Kyle felt there was something familiar about him.

"I must talk to you," said the man. "I saw you go in there and I recognised you."

"You recognised us?" demanded Kyle. "How can that be, we've never met?"

"No, we haven't," agreed the man. "But I know who you are."

Kyle felt a twinge of worry. The man seemed desperate but there was a ring of truth in his voice. "So who are we?" he asked.

"I don't know the woman," the man muttered. "But you, you must be one of the royal family of Yshan."

Shock ran through Kyle. *How had he been recognised?*

"How do you know that?" he demanded.

"Because you look like me."

"What?" exclaimed Kyle.

"He's right," broke in Martina. "You do look similar."

"You've got to take me away from here," the man said, fear in his face.

"Why? Who are you?" asked Kyle.

"My name is Omaron Yshan," the frightened man replied.

"What?" snapped Martina. "A descendent of the original Omaron Yshan?"

"No. I am Omaron Yshan."

"You'd better come with us," said Kyle.

Chapter 33

The Admiral stared at the man standing before him.

"You say that you are Omaron Yshan, the uncle of the Princess Sophie with whom you betrayed the Empire?"

The terrified man nodded his head.

"Don't be ridiculous!" snapped the Admiral, rising to his feet. "That man must be about a hundred and fifty years old! You look about forty."

"I am Omaron Yshan," the other repeated.

"Kyle, does anyone else know about this?"

"Only my First Officer, Sir and she's not saying anything. The rest of the crew only know I brought a refugee back with us."

The Admiral turned back to the man standing alone.

"So why have you fled? I gather that you and the current Empress rule the old Empire. You must have wealth beyond imagining and power to match."

"The *current* Empress?" Omaron said with a cold smile. "This is the same Sophie. There have been no others. And she's quite mad. Somehow she got the idea that I was in contact with her twin brother and was conspiring against her for a return of the Yshan Royal Family. Once she'd decided that, my life was worthless."

The Admiral seemed to think for a quiet moment.

"Let's imagine for just a minute that this insane story is true," he said. "How do you explain your age?"

"The Star," said the man. "The Dark Star. This is one of the rewards I get for serving it."

"The Dark Star?" Kyle jumped to his feet. "It's a Dark Star? We knew you had a Star, but not one that was different from our original. And it supports you and Sophie the way the Star of the Yshan Kings guided us?"

The man nodded again.

"Where did that come from?" demanded the Admiral.

"The Aliens took me to see it when they first got me to help them."

The shocked silence in the room lasted for over a minute. Then Kyle's immobility was shattered.

"Sir, your medallion!" he exclaimed.

The Admiral stared down and then back at Kyle.

"And yours," he said.

The tiny spark on both medallions had turned into a deeper, larger and brighter glow.

"We need to have a meeting of the families," said the Admiral.

* * *

The two Great Families of the new Yshan System met infrequently, only when major events or dangers occurred. In the last ten years, such meetings had been only once a year and then had been mainly administrative as few dangers had threatened the system of sixty prosperous planets, all self-governed and looking to the central planet known for barely-understood reasons as "Henry," only as a figurehead for the Commonwealth of Planets.

Traditionally, chairmanship of the meetings alternated between the senior members of each family. As the technical leader of the Yshans, Kyle was entitled to take the chair this time. However, given the critical subject of this meeting, he had asked Fleet Admiral Bradshaw to run the meeting.

Kyle looked around the table. He knew all the people there, but not all were close acquaintances. Many, but not all were also Fleet Officers, a common career path for people in what were in practice, the two Royal Families of the people. Josh Bradshaw 5th, the son of the Admiral and father of the young pilot who had flown the frigate to safety was an academic, a highly regarded historian at the city's University but not a man with the charisma and energy that both his father and his son displayed.

Sitting next to the middle Bradshaw was another one in the line, the professor's daughter and elder sister of the pilot, another Charlotte, as was the tradition of the first-born daughter of the Bradshaw line who was also given a middle name of Foster. She looked nothing like her namesake as she was not a descendant of the first Charlotte Foster but Kyle found her immensely attractive and occasionally had day-dreams of another Charlotte-Kyle Yshan wedding.

"Good morning, everybody," the Admiral said with a smile and received a polite chorus from the eighteen people round the table in his office.

"Three days ago," continued the Admiral, "Commander Kyle Yshan returned from a spying mission to the heart of the enemy system, our old Home Planet. He returned with the same observations that similar missions have provided, stories of poverty, deprivation and tyranny under the alien occupiers with another Princess Sophie apparently in nominal charge as Empress. We have assumed that she is a descendent of the Sophie who allied with aliens in the act of treason that destroyed the first Yshan Empire, although we can't find any records that suggest a family line from that Sophie."

He looked around the table, making eye contact with each of the persons sitting there. He clearly had their deep attention.

"As you know, the Commander was able to persuade an alien cruiser to come back with him..." He paused as the wave of laughter ran round the group. "And that has undoubtedly saved us from disaster, as we learnt that our old disrupter torpedoes no longer work as they did in the first Battle of Home

Planet when those missiles cancelled all engine and weapons systems in the alien ships."

He paused again and saw that he still had the absolute attention of everybody in the room.

"But the Commander brought back something else," he continued. "This man."

A holographic image of the prisoner appeared in the middle of the table. Everybody's attention switched to the image.

"He claims to be Omaron Yshan," said the Admiral and stopped as a wave of shock and derision ran through the group.

"But let me stress," he continued. "Not a descendent of the original traitor, Omaron Yshan, Uncle of Princess Sophie and Prince Kyle, but *THE* Omaron Yshan himself."

The sounds around the group reflected a mixture of astonishment, disgust and mostly disbelief.

"Josh, that's got to be rubbish!" exclaimed Charlie Bradshaw, the Admiral's sister. "That original Omaron has got to be over a hundred and fifty years old! This one looks about thirty, maybe forty. Now I know that the Yshans live longer than the human line, but not *that* much longer!"

"Exactly what we thought," agreed the Admiral. "So we did some searching in the archives and we found the recording of the trial for treason of Omaron. Here it is."

The image of the prisoner was moved to the side

of the room and a new image appeared. It was a scene of the trial conducted some hundred and twenty years ago, just weeks before the alien invasion of the Empire. It showed Omaron Yshan, still a prince of the Royal Yshan family, standing in the dock before the tribunal of senior Fleet officers.

A murmur of interest ran around the table. "Look at the group in the background," said the young Lieutenant Josh Bradshaw. "That's the first Josh, the first Kyle, and..."

"Good Heavens!" exclaimed the elder Charlie. "That's my namesake, Charlie Foster!"

"And mine, too, Auntie!" added the younger Charlotte."

"And that's Emperor Garamax 19th," said Kyle, pointing to the slender, fair-haired young man. "So who is the other woman? She's in Fleet uniform but I can't see the rank."

"That's my predecessor," said Admiral Bradshaw softly. "That's Captain Kandria Sestucal before she took the others to Earth at the Emperor's orders just before the alien invasion and saved all their lives."

"This is quite fascinating, but we've forgotten the main point of showing this scene," said Kyle. "Look at the man in the dock. Is that the same man as we brought back here?"

For a few moments, everybody stared at the two images and the shock in the room was profound.

"It's the same man," said Charlie. "That's Omaron Yshan, still about forty years old."

"But Charlie, there's a problem," said Kyle. These meetings were informal. "That's certainly the man I brought back but he looks some years older than when we met him last week. I thought he looked younger than me at that point."

A murmur of interest ran round the table.

"Could that be just because of the fear and worry he's experiencing?" asked the elder Charlie.

"I'm sure that's a factor," replied Kyle. "But if he's telling us the truth and something has kept him young, then the possibility exists that the young, beautiful and evil Empress Sophie of today is the same woman who betrayed the Empire a hundred and twenty years ago."

Into that frozen scene of horror, dismay and shock, something happened that blew everything else into far less importance.

The images vanished. Instead, standing just a metre or two from the conference table a tall young woman appeared. She looked about forty, smartly dressed in Fleet uniform but without badges of rank. She smiled at the expressions around the table.

"Good morning," she said. "My name is Kandria Sestucal. I think you just recognised me in that historical scene."

The profound silence in the room lasted for over a minute. Everybody around the table knew the name of this tall young woman. It was engraved in their history and all the legends of how they found on Earth, the Prince Garamax as a young child who knew nothing of his nature and destiny. It was this woman who had led the single battle cruiser against the combined fleet of the Alien Invader and defeated them with the help of the first Josh Bradshaw, Kyle Yshan and the father of the first Charlie Foster. Later still, she was the first Admiral of the New Yshan Fleet after the flight from the Old Empire.

"Admiral Sestucal, I believe?" said the senior Josh Bradshaw, rising to his feet.

The woman smiled at him and waved him to sit down again.

"No longer an Admiral," she said. "That's your role."

"But you are that person?" insisted the Admiral, remaining on his feet. His voice was calm and controlled but Kyle thought he detected a trace of tension in the old man.

"I am," said the woman.

"In that case, you would have to be about a hundred and fifty years old," continued the Admiral. "And you still look like the pictures show you from over a century ago. So you are not Yshan. And you cannot be Human. What *are* you, Kandria Sestucal?"

She smiled again. "I think you already know, Admiral," she replied.

"You are one of the First," said Kyle, at last finding his own voice.

She turned to him, her smile even wider.

"It's so good to see you, Kyle," she said. "You look so like your ancestor, you could be his twin. And of course, you are quite correct. I am one of the First."

The Admiral sat down as if his legs had failed him.

"Why?" he demanded.

"The Yshan people need us again," the woman said. "And we need the Yshan people. We are all in great danger."

Chapter 34

Slowly, the room returned to a normal state but the after-effects of the shock remained as if a stun-grenade had gone off some moments before.

"You'd better explain," said the Admiral.

Kandria Sestucal walked to the head of the table.

"You all know your history," she began. "You know how the Yshan people were dying, starving on a world that itself was dying over five thousand years ago. We appeared then and gave the Star to the first Garamax Yshan. But you need to know, it was not just our wish to save a dying people. That planet had been our home for many hundreds of thousands of years before that, but my people had begun preparations for growing to a new stage of existence in a new, higher dimension. We needed to leave the world to somebody who would take care of it, because we still depend on the health of our planet of origin for our survival. I will explain this more at another time. But now you must understand that the world is again dying under the tyranny of Empress Sophie and her allies, the aliens who drove out the Yshan people."

She looked around the table. Every face was fixed on her.

"We must go to war again," she said. "But first, I must take the descendants of those who started this adventure so many years ago and we must go back to where it all began. There is something there I must show you and that we need. It will be vital for our battle to reclaim the Yshan Empire."

Again, she looked around the table. She moved just a little to the elderly Charlotte, the sister of the Fleet Admiral.

"Charlie, will you give me your medallion?" she asked.

Without hesitation, Charlie lifted the medallion from around her neck and handed it over. Like those around the necks of Fleet Admiral Bradshaw and the young Kyle Yshan, it was glowing with a bright, beautiful light, unlike the almost invisible gleam that all three medallions had shown for the last century or more.

"And yours, Admiral," continued Kandria and again received the medallion without hesitation. She walked around to the youngest Josh Bradshaw and handed one to him. Astounded, he slipped the chain over his head and stared down at the silver disk.

"You also look so like your ancestor, Josh," Sestucal said softly. "And now you, Charlie," she continued and advanced on the younger Charlotte. "Time for you to take your place in history," she said and handed the medallion to the young woman who slowly put it around her neck, staring entranced at the glowing particle.

"We four must go back to where it all began," said Sestucal. "It is right that the youngest of the two families be part of this. What we do back on Earth will let us take back the old Empire."

Chapter 35

"Earth!" exclaimed Charlie. "I never knew it was so beautiful!"

They looked down at the blue, cloud-flecked planet slowly rotating beneath them.

"Nor me," said Josh, not failing to keep some tears running down his cheeks. "It's where we came from, it's the planet of our family's birth! This is my second visit and it still affects me like this."

"Where's Australia?" asked Kyle, also quite affected by the beauty of the planet Earth.

Josh pointed at the southern continent just appearing out of the night shadow on the left and emerging into clear sunlight over the whole country.

"Kandria, can you put us down in the right place?" asked Kyle.

Since leaving the home world, the three of them had slowly become accustomed to dealing with the one-time Fleet Admiral as a friend, but the awe they felt in the presence of one of the legendary "First" remained.

"Of course," she replied and her fingers ran over the computer panels as if testing the texture of a fine silk. "We're fully cloaked, so no Earth radar systems or telescopes will see us."

The three young people watched as the globe seemed to zoom closer and become a vast plain with the deep blue of the sea down the East coast and that vanished as the ship landed in a clearing in the middle of dense woodland.

"Welcome to Earth!" said Kandria as the door opened on one side.

All of them moved to the opening and stood, staring. They had all visited other planets in the Yshan Confederation and Kyle and Josh had visited their old Yshan Capital as spies, so there was no great shock in standing on a new planet under a different sun, but Earth was different. It was the home planet of Charlie's family and the Bradshaws, part of the legends taught to all schoolchildren and it was also the planet where the last Emperor, Garamax 19th had been found as a small child, quite unaware of his true nature and destiny. Only Josh had been here before, visiting to research the Bradshaw family history.

"What is that incredible noise?" exclaimed Charlie as a loud, whooping cackle began somewhere in the woods and was answered by several others around the forest.

"It's called a Kookaburra!" replied Kandria with a smile. "One of Australia's greatest symbols."

"What is it?" asked Charlie, looking nervous. "Is it an animal big enough to eat us?"

Kandria laughed. "It's a bird, Charlie! And one of my favourites! Come on, let's take a walk."

At last, they descended onto the green surface of the woods.

"This is lovely!" said Charlie. "The air is so fresh. I think I like it here!"

"Your ancestors had a property very near here. Yours too, Josh," said Kandria. "And as children, Josh, Henry and Charlie went to school, just about five kilometres away. We'll go and visit soon but there's something here you have to see."

Without any movement being seen, several people appeared in the clearing. All three of the young people let out a gasp.

"Nothing to worry about," said Kandria. "These are my people. These are the First."

*　*　*

Charlie was the first to recover some sort of control. But even then, her voice was raspy with shock and she held her hands before her mouth almost in prayer.

"You are the First? The people that gave us the Star and saved the Yshan race from extinction?"

A tall, dark-haired, distinguished-looking man nearest to her replied.

"We are. It was my grandfather who gave the first Yshan the Star over five thousand years ago."

"Your... your *grandfather?*" said Josh, his voice almost a croak. "I think this is more than I can handle. How old *are* you?"

The man smiled. "I'm just a kid," he said. "Just over a thousand years."

Kandria broke into the conversation, seeing the shock in the eyes of all three of the visitors.

"Let's talk about it over breakfast," she said. "Come, I'd like to show you where we live."

She led the way into the denser wooded area and to a small hut. She opened the door to reveal a staircase.

"The hut is cloaked normally," she said. "Nobody can ever see it and even if they approached too close, we have a mechanism that will make them walk away without realising why. Our ship is protected the same way."

She began walking down the staircase, followed by everybody else.

Josh was feeling real concerns now. This did not feel like the residence of a group of people with the powers that the First had demonstrated.

But as he reached lower down the steps, the view changed his mind.

He was looking out at a beautiful and vast room, much like a ballroom of some luxurious Palace. It seemed to stretch in all directions and although he could see no light sources, the entire place was lit with a soft white glow that seemed quite even throughout.

"Wow!" he gasped and saw the same reaction in his two companions. They continued to the floor and looked around them as the others gradually came down the steps.

Although the room was underground, it seemed to be lined with windows that looked out onto glorious scenes of mountains and lakes. The ceilings were high, covered in beautiful paintings.

"This is where we live," said Kandria, breaking into the silent wonderment.

Josh looked back at the people who had followed them down, including the one man who had spoken to them so far. There seemed to be about thirty or so.

"Where are the rest of you?" Charlie asked, also looking back at the group.

"This is it," said Kandria. "This is all of us who are still left in a physical state."

Charlie took a deep breath.

"You said something like that back at the family meeting. What does it mean?"

Kandria nodded with understanding.

"We'll explain everything to you soon. But now we're going to have a nicely extended and very social breakfast and then later we'll tell you the whole story of why we saved the Yshan people so long ago and why we must do the same again. But let's get breakfast organised and then I want you to meet somebody."

Charlie smiled, seeing the warmth in Kandria and how it was affecting all her friends.

"Yes, we should have something to eat," she said with a small laugh. "After all, we've travelled over two hundred light years since our last meal!"

The other two joined in her relaxed mood and they began moving to a long dining table set at one side of the room. The tantalising smell of coffee drifted to their noses.

"But who's this little boy?" exclaimed Josh, as a small child appeared from a doorway. "He's the first youngster we've seen here."

The child stopped and stared at the three visitors with a solemn, wide-eyed look. Josh estimated he was about seven years old, almost skinny in his build, with fair hair. The boy went to Kandria and she placed a gentle hand on his shoulder.

"This is really whom you have come to meet," she said. "Your ancestors, the first Kyle, Josh and Charlie met him very close to here and they knew him as Henry. Let me present to you the Emperor Garamax 19th, seventy-second Emperor of the Yshan Galactic Empire."

Chapter 36

Breakfast was indeed leisurely, friendly and delicious. Food of every conceivable style was laid out in large bowls on the table and people took what they wanted, as and when they wanted. Tea and coffee seemed never-ending.

Josh was delighted to see his favourite dish of light, thin pancakes served with lemon and sugar, Charlie experimented and found some Asian dishes with an aroma of saffron and Kyle settled for a traditional Australian feast of bacon and eggs and hash brown potatoes.

"And now for some explanations," said Kandria as the meal ended. "Let's go to another room. Henry, will you come with us?"

The small boy followed them without a sound. He had not uttered a word since his appearance and had tucked into his own meal of toast and jam and milk, looking quite calm and self-possessed in the room full of adults.

Kandria led them into a lounge room. Armchairs were placed around the room on a deep red carpet, small coffee tables sat by each chair and the room was pleasantly warm. Drapes of various colours lined the walls. Josh thought this was quite luxurious.

"Take seats," suggested Kandria and took one herself while the others sat in places so that they could look at each other. Little Henry sat cross-legged at Kandria's feet and looked calmly at each of them. Josh felt almost un-nerved at the intense gaze, feeling the boy was reading his very soul. He smiled at him and was pleased to get a small smile in return.

"It really is Garamax," broke in Kandria.

"But how?" demanded Charlie. "The Emperor was murdered well over a century ago, poisoned by Sophie just before he left for the trip here with you and our ancestors."

"Good heavens!" exclaimed Kyle. "I've just realised! We're the same people, just later generations of that original group! Except for you, of course, Kandria! You were one of the group that actually came here with the first Kyle, Josh and Charlie."

"And Henry!" added Josh, unable to stop grinning at the same realisation.

"Yes, Henry," said Charlie. "How on *EARTH* can this be the original Henry?"

"Have you ever seen a recording of his coronation?" asked Kandria.

"I'm pretty sure we all have," answered Kyle.

"Then do you remember this bit?" continued Kandria.

The room darkened a little and in the middle appeared a holographic image of the stage of the coronation so long ago.

Henry was fifteen years old. His uncle, Karocarl, Kyle's father had been filling the position as Regent Emperor while the search for the boy continued and Henry had been found on Earth. Sitting at the rear of the stage were fifteen-year old Kyle, his mother, Josh, Charlie who was about twelve years old and Charlie's mother and father.

The Emperor Karocarl went to the stand on which was placed the Star of the Yshan Kings, the sentient crystal that had guided the Yshan Royal Family for five thousand years. The Emperor picked it up and handed it to Henry. The boy raised the crystal above his head and it immediately glowed with the light of the entire Galaxy, the sure sign that Henry was the rightful Emperor.

"But this is the critical part," broke in Kandria. "This is the second part of the coronation that has never been understood. Watch."

On the stage, the now ex-Emperor replaced the Star on its stand. He bent down behind it and brought out a circular tray that looked like black basalt. On it was a golden mask. To Josh, it looked like something he had seen in his studies of Earth, the mask of an ancient Egyptian Pharaoh, perfect in its pure lines.

"The final sign," murmured Kandria. "The rightful heir must put on the mask and it will take on the features if he's the right one. We've never known until recently where that Mask came from or how it does what it does."

Henry held up the mask for all to see then carefully slipped it against his face. Almost immediately, the metal seemed to flow like mercury, taking on the shape of Henry's face until it looked just like a golden replica of the new Emperor.

Charlie let out a small sigh. "That's the part that still blows me away! I can never get used to it and I've never understood it."

"We discovered only after we came here that it was something the Star created," said Kandria. "It was a form of insurance against exactly the events that did occur, Sophie's murder of the rightful Emperor. What the mask was doing there was literally taking a complete copy of Henry, his mind, his DNA, everything."

Josh suddenly gasped as he realised what she was saying. "So this is a clone of the original Henry?" he exclaimed.

"More than a clone," replied Kandria. "No, this IS Henry. He has been rebuilt from the blueprint the mask was holding."

"But he's only a little boy!" said Kyle. "Henry was about twenty six when he was murdered."

"And this child is a new-born infant," replied Kandria. "He appeared just a year ago as a brand new baby and that's what alerted us to the fact that the time for retaking the Yshan Empire is coming. The mask is gradually growing him back to that stage. Even after the coronation, it stayed linked to Henry's mind and stored all his memories right up to his death. In another few weeks, this little boy will be the fully grown Emperor Garamax 19th with all his memories and all the training and experiences he had before."

Josh, Charlie and Kyle stared at little Henry who looked calmly back.

Josh took a deep breath and turned his gaze to Kandria.

"What did you mean about the First coming here to Earth? Just why are you all here?"

"A perceptive question," said Kandria. "I've said before, we are bound closely to the planet. The world on which we grew, as did the Yshan people, is not just a lump of rock, it has an awareness, a life force. We are part of it, just as you are. But we had to leave when the Star died and the Aliens took over or we too would have died as the planet began dying."

"The *planet* would die?" Charlie's face showed the same enormous shock that Josh felt at those words.

Kandria nodded. "The Aliens are not new to us. They had nearly destroyed us before, an enormously evil force that we do not understand at all. They would have killed off the planet's life force, just as they are doing now. So we came to Earth, a planet much like our home planet, with its own life force in which we can survive. The Human race has also depended on that force for its survival."

All three of the young people were silent for a moment as they tried to digest this information.

"Back at the family meeting," Kyle said, "you said something about the Yshans needing the First and the First needing the Yshans. And you also said you needed the planet for your survival. You've just explained some of that, but it's time you explained the rest of it."

"Very soon," said Kandria. "First, we need to take a short trip outside. Something important is happening."

She stood up and led the way out of the room, down a corridor and opened a door at one end. The others followed her in and were astonished to see several ground vehicles parked in a garage.

Kandria saw the looks of astonishment and laughed.

"Sometimes, even The First need to go shopping!" she said. "We go into town just like any of the locals!"

They piled into a capacious station wagon with Henry sitting next to Kandria, inseparable as always and Charlie next to him in the front seat. Kyle and Josh took the back seats as the car pulled out into sunlight of a beautiful, sunny day.

Two or three kilometres along a quiet road, Kandria pointed to an attractive farmhouse a few hundred metres from the road.

"That was the Foster family home," she said. "That was where Charlie first took Kyle, Sophie and Josh horse riding and Charlie's mother realised that the twins were not human."

Charlie wiped a tear from her eyes. That story was all part of the collection of legends taught to all schoolchildren in the Yshan worlds

After a few more minutes of silence, the car drove slowly past the grounds of a school building.

"Is that..." asked Josh, fascinated.

Kandria nodded. "Yes, that's the school," she said. "Right there by the gate is where Kyle and Josh practiced their unarmed combat and where Omaron and one of his thugs attacked them to their great cost."

"Of course, you actually saw that fight!" said Josh. "You were there!"

"I was Miss Hickey, the new teacher," replied Kandria. "Sent by the Fleet Admiral to protect Kyle and Sophie against just that threat. But as it turned out, Sophie was part of the threat."

"This is incredible," said Kyle. "All these stories, they're so bound up in our history. To see the places where they happened, it's astonishing."

The three visitors stared at the building. Pictures of the school were common in the history books of the Yshan people of the new Commonwealth and this scene was well known. There were two new buildings to one side and on the other, a large greenhouse had been constructed.

"It's amazing!" said Josh. "Over a century later, it still looks much the same, just like any school anywhere else in the country!"

"And I bet the classrooms are still like they were," agreed Charlie. "Hey, look, a couple of kids! They're wearing the same uniform our namesakes wore!"

But Kandria was staring at something else. Two people were standing by the school gate, looking with concentration at the car and its occupants.

"Who are they?" asked Charlie. "They're weird! I've never seen anyone so tall!"

"We knew they'd find us some day," muttered Kandria.

"Who?" asked Kyle.

"Aliens," Kandria replied. "They've been looking for us since the invasion and they must have picked up rumours of our presence here. We first detected them a few days ago. That's why this is happening, why Henry's rebirth occurred and why I came to get you. Whatever life force of the Star remains must have detected their arrival."

"Aliens?" snapped Kyle. "Do they know who we are?"

"They know who I am, certainly," said Kandria. "So they may be able to work out who you are. We need to get back to the base."

She accelerated and drove round the corner, returning to the main road and ten minutes later they were back underground in the secret location.

"What now?" asked Kyle as they took their seats again in the room where they had been earlier. "How long before we must leave?"

"Not long," replied Kandria. "There's no doubt the aliens will report back to their base, but they can't be certain about your identities and they have no indications of where you came from. But it could be some days before they do anything about it."

"What will they do, do think?" asked Josh.

"Probably send a military squad to attack this base," replied Kandria.

"Can you defend it?" asked Kyle. "I'm pretty sure you have some good weapons."

"It's not a problem," replied Kandria with a smile.

"Then is it time to tell us how all this began and how the Star appeared?" asked Charlie.

"Indeed it is," said Kandria.

Chapter 37 - The Very Distant Past

The planet was called Yggrandal by its people. They had enjoyed many thousands of years of peace, wealth and a passion for exploring their world and learning of its mysteries and beauties.

Now it was a time of crisis.

Only months before, an alien species had appeared in their skies, in ships far advanced on the technology of Yggrandal. No communication had taken place but the aliens simply destroyed towns and cities and set up mining operations in many areas, taking minerals from the land and leaving devastation in place of beauty.

Now there was just hunger and disease as the population declined by many thousands every day.

"We are nearly at the end," said Emorill. By acclaim, he was the leader of what had once been a global government, a group selected by lottery from its adult citizens every five years.

A wave of sadness swept through the hall. The entire population of the city was here, no more than a thousand people and nobody knew how many, if any remained in the rest of the world. There had been no communications from anywhere on the planet for weeks now.

"And our world also seems to be ending," said a young woman at the front of the crowd. "When we still could talk to people all over the planet, they all told of the plants and animals dying."

A murmur of grief ran through the crowd.

"We and the planet seem to be tied together, somehow," said Emorill. "I think our planet will die when we have gone."

"And we have no idea who these aliens are or where they came from?" asked an elderly man.

Emorill shook his head. "Not from this world, that's all we know for sure. We have never seen one. They remain in their vehicles and destroy all we have ever built."

"Another world!" sighed the young woman who had spoken before. "We have dreamed of such things, told tales to our children, but how horrible that our first contact would lead to our destruction."

Silence fell in the hall. Everybody there knew that their lives were coming to an end soon. The strange ships had appeared over the city in the last two weeks and already the damage had been horrendous. The attacks were carried out without any apparent pattern, just a child's eager destruction of everything standing.

A small light appeared in the space between

Emorill and the crowd. Instinctively, people moved away, giving the light more space but there seemed no fear in the room as if the light emitted a calming influence. It grew stronger and with it sounded a low, musical note like a cathedral organ playing softly.

The light seemed to spin, beams flashed out from the centre of it and then it faded. There was a huge, collective gasp as the people saw a man standing there.

"It's time we met," said the man. "There is much to do."

He looked like any man in the hall. He was of medium height, stocky build, dressed in simple attire much like everybody else and he carried a bag over his shoulders which he placed on the floor. And yet there was something about him, a power of personality that shone out over the hall and covered everybody with a protective cloak of love.

"You are right," he said, smiling at the leader, Emorill. "You and the planet are tied together. You draw on the world's inner powers for your own and at the same time, it needs you to fill its own dreams."

"Who *are* you?" croaked Emorill, the shock taking all strength from him.

"My people are those who preceded you on this world," said the man. "We lived here for nearly eight hundred thousand years, just as you have, peacefully, happily, living closely with the planet's own life force."

Emorill shook his head in confusion. All around

him, the silence was complete. Every face in the room was turned to this mysterious newcomer, but there was no fear in the hall.

The man smiled in sympathy.

"This is hard for you, I know. But what I said is true. We had a full civilisation centuries before your people developed into tribes and when we saw your growth into civilisation, we knew our time to move on had also come."

Still struggling for self-control, Emorill took a deep breath. "Where did you go?" he whispered. "Another world?"

The man shook his head. "Not another world. Another dimension. Just as your people will do some day when you have fully grown and your growth will greatly exceed ours."

"I doubt we will live long enough," said Emorill sadly. "We will probably all die in the next few days."

"If that happens, then the whole world will also die, as one of you has already suggested. And if the world dies, then my people will also die, because we are still a part of this planet, just as you are."

"But how can it be stopped?" demanded Emorill. "These invaders have weapons we cannot even imagine. I think the people in this hall are the last of our kind."

The newcomer shook his head. "And now you have a weapon that will drive them away."

He bent down and opened the bag at his feet, standing up again with what looked like a crystal about the size of his head. It was white and seemed to glow slightly.

"And how will that help us?" demanded Emorill. His whole body radiated disappointment and contempt.

"This crystal contains the minds, the skills, the wisdom and the powers of all my people," replied the mysterious stranger. "First, it needs to find the person in whom it can entrust that wisdom and guide them to lead. It will take care of the aliens in its own way."

"And how will it do that?" asked Emorill, starting to sense some hope that the entire world was not coming to an end after all.

The man came closer to him and held out the crystal. "Take it," he said.

Cautiously, Emorill took the crystal from the stranger. It weighed less than he had expected and he sensed enormous power within it.

"Hold it above your head," the man commanded.

With just a pause, Emorill obeyed, uncertain of what was happening. The crystal hummed with a low note and the gleam increased just enough to be detected but beyond that, nothing strange occurred.

The man smiled and took the crystal back.

"You have been a fine leader," he said. "But you are not the one to return the people to greatness."

He turned and studied the group. In the faces before him, he saw hope, concern, happiness, even some derision. He beckoned to the young woman who had spoken before and she approached, looking nervous.

"You try," said the man, handing her the crystal and she took it gingerly. Immediately it hummed louder and the gleam from inside it grew stronger.

The man gestured at her to hold it up and she did so.

Immediately, the crystal emitted a light that seemed stronger than every sun in the skies, even the whole Galaxy. The light flooded into every corner of the hall, lit up every face and wiped out every shadow.

In the confusion, joy broke out as everybody seemed to recognise that their tragedy had been averted. When they looked around to ask the man what this meant, he had vanished.

Chapter 38

"That was over a million years ago," said Kandria, looking with amusement at the faces around her, utterly enthralled by the story she had been telling.

"But what happened then?" breathed Charlie. She had been entranced by the tale as it unfolded.

"The aliens vanished within weeks," replied Kandria. "It was almost like a long-ago story here on Earth about how the Martians invaded and almost destroyed Earth but fell sick to all of the planet's microbes and germs because they had no immunity. We found no dead specimens, they simply vanished. But our people recovered, began to expand again and as they did, the planet too recovered. The young woman for whom the crystal had glowed remained a leader for over a century. We were already a long-lived race, and we expanded our normal life-times to over two thousand years. And we began to expand outward, too. We had so many of the ships left by the aliens that we were able to develop them for our own use and later design our own space-ships and slowly we built a planetary empire."

"So why are you not still there?" asked Josh. "What happened to you?"

"Did you see the similarity between our tale of getting the crystal and the same legends that the Yshan people have?" asked Kandria.

"Ah! Of course!" said Kyle. "It contained the minds and wisdom of your predecessors. So is that the same crystal that was given to us?"

Kandria shook her head.

"We had the same story as our earlier race. We began to grow out of our physical bodies and into a new dimension. In the last few years of our time on the planet, our crystal began to fade and finally died. The one we gave you contained the same wisdom and minds of most of our own people and there are few of us left now. In time, the same will happen to the Yshan race."

"Kandria," broke in Charlie. "What did you mean about the planet having dreams and a life force? How can a planet be *alive?*"

"Ours is," replied Kandria. "Many planets around the universe are living entities, just as Earth is and the people living on it are part of the life force. If they die, the planet dies and the reverse is also true."

"And the alien presence is killing our world?" asked Charlie.

Kandria nodded. "That is so. The two races are utterly dangerous to each other and it looks like they found their own Star to use as a weapon."

"But our Star is dead!" interjected Kyle.

"And that's why you are here," replied Kandria. "Now it's time for you to prepare to return home with the Emperor and the Star."

"A new Star?" asked Josh. "Are we going to get a new Star somehow?"

Kandria merely smiled, stood up and walked out of the room. The rest of them followed, puzzled.

She led them back to the large hall where they had first arrived. It seemed that the rest of her people were also there. She stopped by the table where they had eaten breakfast earlier, but it was completely clear and shone with a polished wood surface.

"Put your medallions on the table," Kandria said. "Henry, yours too."

The little boy reached inside his shirt and pulled out another medallion identical to the three carried by Josh, Charlie and Kyle. All of them were glowing strongly. Gently, Kandria nudged them until they were touching.

The medallions began to glow more strongly and increased the energy until it was hard to look directly at them.

The gleam became a ball of light over each medallion which expanded until with a soundless flicker, all four sources of light combined as one and then it was too bright to look at. The three friends hid their eyes until they sensed the power of the light had faded and they dropped their hands from their faces.

Sitting on the table, humming gently was a Star.

* * *

All four of them stared at the glowing crystal for several moments.

Josh was the first to look away to make a comment to Kandria but what he saw made him gasp with shock.

Apart from his two friends and the little boy called Henry, the room was empty.

"Where is everybody?" exclaimed Charlie, looking around in bewilderment. "I didn't see anyone leave."

Kyle was smiling with joy. He moved to the table and began stroking his fingertips over the Star. It glowed a little more strongly and hummed, almost like a cat purring.

"They're in here!" he said and picked it up. He turned to the little boy.

"Henry," he said. "I think you know what to do."

"Yes," said the child, the first word he had spoken since they had met him just a few hours before. He lifted the Star above his head.

The light of all the stars in the entire Galaxy seemed to shine from the crystal and illuminated every corner of the huge room.

"Time to go home," said Kyle. "The Emperor must reclaim his Empire."

Chapter 39

"These will completely immobilise the alien ships," said the Chief Engineer at the Gregory Foster Institute of Technology. The building was not huge, though much of it was underground for safety reasons. It was named after the father of the first Charlie Foster, a human who displayed extraordinary genius after being introduced to Yshan science and took it further than anyone could have dreamed.

Commander Kyle Yshan looked at the small torpedo in its frame. It was nothing remarkable in appearance, about a metre long, quite broad and looked more like the pictures Kyle had seen of the blimps used for advertising back on Earth. It was a featureless black with nothing obvious to be seen on the outside.

"How does it do that?" asked Kyle doubtfully.

The engineer laughed. "We've been busy while you've been holidaying back on Earth, Commander," he said. "We stripped down the alien ship to every nut and bolt, analysed every computerised part, tested every printed circuit and then did it all again!"

"And did you find out how they'd neutralised the effect of our earlier torpedoes?"

The engineer grinned smugly. He was a tall, middle-aged man with a full head of red hair, an equally bushy, red moustache and the broad-shouldered, lanky build of an athlete, spoiled by a small pot belly under his white laboratory coat.

"We certainly did! They'd developed a doo-hickey that generated a force field that blanked out the ones our torpedoes developed. It was dead easy to build something that would counter that effect."

"And that is what's in the torpedo now?" asked Kyle.

The engineer blew a noisy raspberry. "That would be MUCH too easy," he said. "Give us some credit, Commander, my team is made up of the best theoretical physicists, mathematicians and cosmologists in the Commonwealth. We had that little problem cleared up in a day, so we went quite a bit further."

"And?" inquired Kyle. The engineer's enthusiasm and air of hidden secrets was interesting him. What else did this man have?

"We also looked at the fuel sources," said the other man. "They're a very potent mixture of energy cells and nuclear power that provide enormous energy but tends to be unstable. So they stabilise the mixture with a blanket force field that works very well."

Kyle laughed out loud as he saw where the man was going. "And you found a way of cancelling that force field?"

"We surely did," shouted the engineer, his delight too much to keep under control. "Put one of these babies within a million kilometres of one of their ships and not only will all their systems fail, but their internal power sources will get so unstable, everybody on board will be too occupied trying to stop themselves blowing up to think about fighting!"

Kyle's grin was almost ear to ear. "That's fantastic!" he said. "How soon can you get them into production?"

"Starting today," the engineer replied with a satisfied smile. "We'll have several thousand within a year."

"Your team has certainly earned its keep," said Kyle.

"Like I said, Commander, we're the very best there is. There's more than I've told you."

"Good grief, isn't that enough? You've given us the weapon to defeat those aliens, just like the first Gregory Foster did. What else did you do?"

"We ripped into their navigation system. What we found is the perfect addition to the torpedo mechanisms. We found a transponder system that shows us the location of every ship in their fleet. That's very useful of course, so we built into the torpedo, a system of finding each ship and flying straight there through the nearest wormhole and any others in between. Commander, we can put a torpedo next to every ship in their fleet and we know exactly how many ships they have and where they are."

"How many have you got ready?" asked Kyle.

"Just four," replied the engineer.

"Have they been tested?"

"Not against a real life alien warship," the engineer replied.

"Get them aboard my ship," said Kyle. He touched his communicator.

"Admiral, it's time to go hunting," he said.

Chapter 40 – Alien Hunting

"Report," said Commander Kyle Yshan from his Command Seat on the bridge of his frigate, the Planetary Commonwealth Ship, *"Charlie Foster"* which had just soared through a wormhole after leaving home base eight hours before.

"On target, sir," replied Lieutenant Josh Bradshaw from the pilot's seat. "We're in the Home Galaxy, Sector MPR057, 82,000 light years from Yshan Home World."

"Location of our target?" demanded Kyle.

"Still registering in Sector KLJ098," replied the Navigation Officer who had been given the task of monitoring the system taken from the captured alien battle cruiser. "That's one wormhole transit away, so there's no way we can be detected."

Kyle knew all the data, having developed the battle plan himself but going through the procedures of "Challenge and Verification" as it was known was a security measure and one that enabled all the crew to follow the action.

"Weapons?" said Kyle.

"Weapons, aye," replied a voice through the communications speaker. The Weapons Officer was down in the torpedo room.

"Status?" asked Kyle.

"All four fish armed and ready," replied the Weapons Officer. "The first one is programmed to pass through the wormhole and meet the alien in its present position."

"Thanks, Weapons," replied Kyle. "Nav, ready to follow?"

"Ready, sir," said the Navigations Officer.

"Twenty seconds after the torpedo goes, follow," ordered Kyle.

"Twenty seconds, aye," replied Nav.

"Weapons, first fish, shoot!"

"On its way, sir," said the voice from the torpedo room.

The Bridge was silent as they watched the forward screen. The massive, flaming ring of the wormhole erupted into life as the torpedo raced through and then it faded. In dead silence the officers waited as the countdown continued, then the engines thundered into life and the *"Charlie Foster"* accelerated sharply and went through the wormhole in the identical direction and at the same speed as the torpedo.

"Position!" snapped Kyle.

"Sector KLJ098 on target," replied Nav. "We are less than one million kilometres from the recorded position of the alien cruiser and closing. I have no sign of it, so it's probably cloaked."

"And the fish?"

"Torpedo should ignite in five, four, three, two, one... there she blows!"

In the black distance, a tiny gleam lit up and faded again. In the background of stars, a small circle blacked out a patch of the galaxy's light.

"Its cloaking mechanism has gone," said the Navigation Officer. He couldn't keep the excitement out of his voice. "It's just three hundred thousand kilometres away."

"Stand by regular torpedoes," ordered Kyle. "We don't know if their weapons have been disabled. Josh, take us towards that ship. Be prepared for anything."

"Aye, sir," replied Josh in the pilot's seat.

"Anything showing, Number One?" asked Kyle to his First Officer sitting to his right.

"Checking, sir," she said softly, her eyes intent on the instruments on the small screen beside her. Then she grinned. "They're dead in the water, Skipper," she said. "Nothing's working over there!"

"Keep heading there, Josh," said Kyle. "Everybody, they may look dead, but..."

As he spoke, the space ahead lit up in a furious explosion of energy. The ball of fire expanded to fill the screens and they automatically darkened to protect the eyes of the watchers.

The fire subsided and the screen lightened up again.

"Nothing there, sir," reported the First Officer. "Just dust and a few small bits of debris. It looks like their nuclear cells blew up."

"That destabiliser doo-hickey worked pretty well, then," murmured Kyle. "The engineer will be delighted."

He pressed the communicator button and the face of Fleet Admiral Josh Bradshaw appeared.

"We have a weapon, sir," said Kyle. "The battle cruiser blew up as we approached. It needed just one torpedo."

The relief on the Admiral's face was obvious.

"Well done, everybody," he said. "So the weapon worked and it looks like the alien computer gives us the location of every one of their ships."

"I've got three fish left, sir."

"Happy hunting, Kyle," said the Admiral.

"Thank you, sir," said Kyle. "Navigator? Where's the next alien ship?"

"Two wormhole transits, Skipper, Sector AQJ910. There are two cruisers together."

"Two together, eh?" said Kyle. "Too juicy a target to miss. Feed the coordinates to Weapons, Lieutenant. Weapons, tell me when you have the next two torpedoes programmed."

"Coordinates received, we'll be ready in three minutes."

"I think my long-ago ancestor in that war back on Earth would have said, "Tally Ho!" said Josh. "It's what the fighter pilots said when they saw the enemy aircraft."

"Then Tally Ho it is, Josh!" Kyle could not keep the excitement out of his voice and the atmosphere on the Bridge reflected it.

"Time to reclaim the Empire, then?" asked Josh.

"Time to reclaim the Empire," agreed Kyle.

* * *

On the bridge of the Pfor'Xscur Battle Cruiser, the scene was peaceful. The twin to this cruiser was also in orbit round their home world, just a hundred kilometres away and clearly visible as it moved out of the planet's night shadow and into sunlight.

"Freighters report all loads deposited on the surface, Captain," said the First Officer.

"Good," replied the Captain, stirring in his seat after some hours of watching the convoy of freighters they had escorted from Yshan Home World. "Navigator, set course for base."

A few minutes of silence reigned on the bridge as the ship got under way.

"These convoys are starting to bore me, Number One," said the captain. "We're a warship, and all we do is escort those freighters from that miserable Yshan Planet and back again."

The First Officer didn't smile. "Our people need the minerals we take, sir."

The Captain sighed. "I know, I know, but it's boring all the same. It's not as if the old Yshan fleet still exists and they all seem to have vanished anyway. We're getting rusty like this!"

"I'm not so sure," replied the other officer. "Those reports of one of our ships simply vanishing last year still worry me. They said they were chasing an Yshan frigate and then they disappeared. What could have caused that?"

The Captain shrugged. "More likely their control systems for their fuel cells failed and the ship blew up. Believe me, there's no Yshan Fleet anywhere in the Universe."

At that moment, the lights went out and were immediately replaced by the dim red glow of the emergency back-up lights.

"Report!" shouted the Captain.

"All systems failed," came the voice from the Engineering Deck. "Propulsion is down, life support is down, weapons are down."

"How! How can that happen? Get onto it, get those systems fixed!" The Captain was displaying panic. He was right, over a century of their dominance over the old Yshan Empire had provided not a single need for emergency action at all and they had lost the capacity to deal with it. Even though the mystery of the complete disappearance of the Cruiser many months ago had caused worry in the High Command and there had been not a clue as to the cause of it, nothing else had disturbed the Pfor'Xscur Empire since its successful invasion of the Yshan Galactic Empire and the total disappearance of the Yshan Imperial Fleet.

The panic-stricken voice from Engineering came back on the speaker.

"Sir! Fuel stabilisation has failed. We need to get out of here!"

The Captain decided immediately. "Abandon Ship!" he called. "Abandon Ship!"

That was as far as he got. At that moment, the cruiser was blown into cosmic dust as the fuel systems blew up like a dozen nuclear bombs.

The crew didn't know that the other cruiser a short distance away exploded in the same manner just two seconds later.

Chapter 41

"It's all very confusing," said the tall young man with fair hair. He looked to be in his late twenties.

"I know intellectually that I'm less than two years old, or at least, this *body* is less than two years old," he continued. "But I remember my entire life before, first as Henry then as Emperor Garamax, everything, that is, up to the moment when I died on the ship returning from Earth. The fact that I was murdered by Sophie over a hundred and twenty years ago, that's the thing I have so much difficult grasping."

"I don't think we can have any idea of what you've gone through," said Kyle. "Is there anything we can do?"

Henry smiled. "The Star is giving me a fast education on the history since my murder, so I'm up to date! But Charlie, Josh and Kyle were my best friends back then and they look so much like you do now, I feel you really are the same people."

"But I don't look anything like the original Charlie Foster!" protested Charlie. "I'm a Bradshaw, not a direct descendant of hers at all!"

"Strange, isn't it?" said Henry. "I think my mind is convincing me that you *do* look like her, even though I can see the difference when I look at pictures of the first Charlie. Anyway, it doesn't matter! You three are my friends!"

"And that's our honour," said Josh. "But now we have to get home to our original planet and restore your Empire."

Henry grimaced. "I think the important thing is to get rid of those appalling aliens and restore a decent life for everybody."

"That first," agreed Kyle. "And we need to bring the Empress Sophie to trial. I wonder if she really is the original one?"

"I think so," said Josh. "Omaron Yshan is already looking about sixty years old and aging fast. That Dark Star must be the reason why they stayed so young but now that he's away from its influence, it can't keep him that way."

"Couldn't happen to a nicer man," said Kyle with a grin.

The buzzer on his collar gave a tiny grunt. Kyle listened briefly to a voice in his ear and looked at Josh. Informality was gone, military discipline returned.

"Time to get on board, Lieutenant Bradshaw," he said. "We're off to war."

"Yes, sir," replied Josh.

"And of course I'm coming too," said Galactic Emperor Garamax 19th.

"Of course, Sire," said Kyle. "Your Imperial Fleet is waiting for you."

Chapter 42

"This is the Captain," said Commander Kyle Yshan.

The frigate, the *"Charlie Foster"* hung in space at the very edge of the home galaxy that had been governed by the Yshan Royal Family before the invasion by the alien fleet over a hundred and twenty years ago. Just a few kilometres away, the flagship of the Fleet, the *"Admiral Sestucal"* floated silently, surrounded by many other ships. Aboard the flagship was the Fleet Admiral and with him, the young man who once was the Galactic Emperor and soon would be again.

Within a sealed case was the gleaming crystal, the new Star of the Yshan Kings.

"Time to give you the battle plan briefing," continued Kyle.

* * *

Back in the basements of the Gregory Foster Institute of Technology, the atmosphere was tense but not worried. The scene was much like some pictures that hung on the walls of the old control rooms during the space exploration days on old Earth, nearly two hundred years before, lines of men and women at control screens.

"Each of those one hundred positions is controlling ten torpedoes," said the Chief Engineer, the man who had briefed Kyle Yshan on the capabilities of the new torpedoes. The silent woman standing with him was Charlotte Bradshaw, the elderly sister of the Fleet Admiral and the great aunt of the pilot aboard Kyle's frigate.

"As you know, the captured alien battle cruiser gave us their computers which among all the other wonderful data also gave us the ability to track every single ship in their fleet. We've coded each torpedo with the coordinates of a ship and they are scattered all over their own galaxy and the Yshan galaxy, with only a small fleet surrounding the original Yshan home planet."

"How many ships in all?" asked the elder Charlie.

"Twelve hundred and thirty," replied the engineer. "Of those, three hundred are near the home planet. Our own fleet is six hundred ships and they are armed with six torpedoes each."

"So what's going to happen?" asked the elderly woman. She was ten years older than the Admiral but like her brother, full of energy and equipped with a powerful brain. She was, in fact, the top mathematician at the Institute and had played a significant part in designing the new torpedoes.

"It's all in the timing," said the engineer. "Those people at their terminals have already launched their torpedoes and right now, the computers are plotting the exact positions of each of the alien ships and the time taken for the torpedoes to reach their wormholes and then the target ships. They will all have to be despatched at different times to hit their targets at exactly the same moment. So a thousand torpedoes have targeted all the alien ships that are away from the home planet."

"And the fleet around the home planet?" asked Charlie.

"Same thing. Our fleet will fire their torpedoes at their own targets and go through the wormholes and arrive around the home planet all at the same moment. Every alien ship should be destroyed within a second or two of each other."

"And it's all up to the computers now, is it?"

"Yes it is. Things should start happening in about twenty minutes."

The two senior scientists shook hands.

"See you back on Home World of the new Yshan Empire," said Charlie.

"You bet!" said the engineer.

* * *

"So it's all up to the computers," said Kyle, finishing his briefing to the crew. "The fleet will move through the wormhole and make three more jumps through further wormholes to arrive at Home World, all automatically controlled by the computers. We will release our torpedoes at exactly the same moment all the torpedoes controlled on the ground at the Institute basement will hit theirs located away from Home World. We will follow the torpedoes through the final wormhole and arrive at Home World a few seconds after the torpedoes have struck. We have nearly twice as many ships as the aliens and we have six torpedoes each, with one programmed to a specific target, in our case a frigate about the same size as us, and two others programmed to alternate targets. The rest can be fired should we need them for any other convenient target we may see or as back-ups for the others. So man your stations, monitor everything and be prepared to take manual control in case anything goes wrong. We'll be moving off in about fifteen minutes. To your stations, everybody."

All around the ship, the crew of thirty-three officers and men and women went calmly about their duties. If any of them showed nerves or fear, the well-disciplined professionals hid it, taking their lead from the complete composure of their Captain and Bridge Officers.

The Weapons team checked their new torpedoes again, checked their conventional high-explosive torpedoes should they be needed and made sure there were no loose objects that could fly around and cause damage in the event of high-stress manoeuvres.

The Navigator checked for the tenth time that he had the coordinates of their first, second and third alternate targets and that they had been correctly fed to the Weapons team.

Josh tested his controls that he'd had modified by the ship's engineer to resemble the controls of a conventional fighter plane of an earlier age back on Earth. He'd become so hooked on the fighter techniques of that time and of the war in which his ancestor had flown a Hurricane that he felt more comfortable and more in control with the old "stick and rudder" system than with the standard methods. Also linked to his control were the massive cannons that fired explosive shells, a weapon very rarely used.

Kyle sat calmly in his Captains chair, sipping at a mug of coffee. His stomach was churning and he was sure that was true of everybody else aboard the ship, but keeping a calm, controlled air was essential for a ship's Captain.

"Fleet's moving, sir," said the First Officer softly. "First wormhole transit in eight minutes."

Kyle touched the ship-wide communications button on his seat's arm.

"All right, everybody, we're moving. We'll be in action very soon. Like our young pilot says, "Tally Ho!" and let's get those aliens out of our home."

Chapter 43

Within seconds the entire fleet had passed through the wormhole, the first of three between their position and the final lap to the home planet.

"On target, in sector, KLS871," reported the Navigator. "The fleet is together. Next wormhole in fourteen minutes."

Nobody had anything to do except monitor their equipment. The entire flight was controlled by computer as the complete fleet had to arrive in the final sector and fire their torpedoes within fractions of a second of each other, just as the torpedoes being controlled back at the Technical Institute had to meet their targets in the aliens' home galaxy simultaneously to avoid those ships giving the alarm before they were destroyed.

"Next wormhole transit, on my mark, twenty seconds," reported the Navigation Officer.

Kyle nodded to signify he had heard. His throat felt dry and he didn't feel like speaking.

The ring of fire erupted ahead and the fleet went soaring through.

"On target, in sector, VBS650," reported the Navigator. "The fleet is together. Next wormhole in twenty-one minutes."

Kyle tensed a little. The computers had programmed a torpedo to be released by each ship and go through the last wormhole twenty seconds ahead of the fleet. If all went to plan, the fleet would find nothing but debris when they arrived, but Kyle remembered something that had been taught at the Fleet Academy.

"A battle plan lasts only until the first shot has been fired."

"Torpedo away," reported the Navigation Officer. A few seconds later, the fire ring of the wormhole burst into life.

"Ten seconds," said the Navigation Officer hoarsely, not able to control the nerves completely.

"Battle Stations," ordered Kyle and the sirens went off to alert the entire crew.

The fire ring approached and the screen showed a number of other ships of the fleet already going through on their computer-controlled paths and then the *"Charlie Foster"* was through as well.

The space on the other side of the wormhole was utter chaos. Debris lay everywhere and without the protective shields, collisions with huge chunks of metal would have destroyed the frigate in seconds.

Kyle couldn't help the overwhelming shock he felt. The scene of devastation reminded him that more than three hundred ships had been destroyed and with them their crews. Kyle had no love for the species that had invaded his Empire and treated the citizens of the Yshan Galaxy with such cruelty, but still... several thousand intelligent beings had just died and he could not avoid feeling the horror.

"Sir! Incoming!" shouted the First Officer as the screen showed a tiny spark approaching the frigate. Kyle had no time to call to Josh for evasive action but Josh didn't need the order. The engines bellowed into life under intense acceleration and the frigate rolled over and dived sharply, rolled again and climbed back, reversed direction and pointed at the source of the enemy torpedo which had flashed by, missing the frigate by a hundred metres and disappearing.

"You have control, Josh," said Kyle belatedly.

There was no reply from the pilot. He was busily hauling the ship into a tight loop that would have crushed the crew had it not been for the gravity controls.

"There it is!" reported the First Officer. "Its shields must be down, but somehow one of the torpedoes didn't function properly. It's still alive."

"Got it," said Josh more to himself. He centred the alien ship in his sights and flung the *"Charlie Foster"* at the target. At the last second, the enemy ship rolled tightly and pulled away, looped upward and tried to come in behind the frigate.

"This bloke's good!" muttered Josh. "We seem to be in an actual dogfight!"

He rolled rapidly, several times and then pulled down in an inverted loop, rolled again and pulled back up, slapped the throttles shut and the enemy ship raced underneath him, clearly confused by the manoeuvre. Josh pushed the stick forward, brought the enemy vessel back into his sights and closed up to within just a few hundred metres.

The other ship desperately threw itself around, trying to shake the frigate off its tail, but Josh concentrated fiercely, gradually reducing the distance between the two, not at all aware of the dead silence on the bridge as everybody watched this incredible battle.

Josh took one hand off the throttle and touched his gun control. Four immensely powerful cannons roared, their sound audible on the bridge. Streaks of red tracer shells hurtled toward the enemy ship and then in a soundless blast it blew itself into dust.

"Gotcha!" said Josh and pulled the ship around the explosion.

Kyle realised he hadn't taken a breath for some time and relaxed with an explosive gasp, echoed by almost every other person on the bridge.

"Great flying, Josh," he said, trying to calm the thumping of his heart.

Josh didn't answer. He had slumped down in his seat, clearly drained by the sudden demands that had been placed on him.

"Medic to the Bridge!" called Kyle and nodded at his First Officer. "Take over Josh's place, will you, Number One? Locate the flagship and get us alongside."

Two officers pulled Josh from his seat and laid him out on the floor as a medical officer arrived and began to examine him.

"The Admiral on fleet broadcast," reported the Navigation Officer as the Admiral's face appeared on the screen. He looked sombre.

"I can report the complete destruction of the alien fleet," the older man said, his voice reflecting tension and fatigue. "Not only here around Home World, but the Institute has reported total success with the remotely fired torpedoes. There is not a single enemy ship left in action. Not all of them blew up but all of them have lost their propulsion and weapons systems and the crews have had to evacuate and take refuge on any possible planets nearby as their life support systems also failed."

The old man had to stop and wipe tears from his eyes.

"I am about to take Emperor Garamax 19th down to the home world," he continued. "Commander Kyle Yshan, please have Lieutenant Bradshaw and yourself join us."

"You bet sir," muttered Kyle, so softly that the Admiral couldn't hear him.

"The Lieutenant is fine, sir," reported the medical office attending Josh. "But that episode drained him like a squeezed sponge! He's fit and strong, give him twenty minutes or so."

Behind him, Josh was sitting up and looking around. His face was white.

Kyle let out a laugh. "Your however-many-greats grandfather back on Earth would have been proud of you, Josh!" he said. "That was superb flying!"

"It just goes to show you, sir," said Josh. "Some things never change, but who would have thought a fighter pilot of two hundred years ago would have shown us how to defeat an enemy space-ship?"

"Get yourself ready, Lieutenant Bradshaw," said Kyle. "We have a date with an Empress."

Chapter 44 - The Empress Sophie

A fleet of thirty-two shuttlecraft descended to the city that had once been the Capital of the Yshan Galactic Empire. One of them contained the Admiral, Josh, Kyle and Charlie who had finally persuaded the Admiral to let her come along. It also contained Emperor Garamax 19th who had been on the throne of the Yshan Empire until murdered by his cousin Sophie when the aliens had invaded and placed her on the throne instead.

The Emperor, now fully restored in appearance to the tall, handsome young man with a charismatic face that he had been, stood before the viewing screen gazing out at the city. His hand rested on the metal case that held the Star.

The view outside was not impressive. The city had been allowed to degenerate over the century or more that the aliens had ruled and the buildings and roads all showed the decay.

As the final shuttle touched down, the Admiral rose to his feet.

"Send out the troops first," he said. "The enemy may still be around and I want no more shocks."

The shuttle pilot, a Captain of the fleet nodded and spoke briefly into his communications system. The doors to the other shuttles opened and armed troops raced out or drove out on armoured personnel carriers. They began dispersing through the city while two large groups made for the Royal Palace. Four armed men in full battle equipment stayed in the shuttle.

The Fleet Captain remained at his position in the pilot's chair, listening intently to the reports from his troops.

"No sign of the enemy at all, sir," he said at one point. "The Palace detail has now entered the building. No sign of life at all."

"Thank you, Captain," said the Admiral.

Another ten minutes passed before the Captain spoke again.

"Civilians, sir!" he said. "They've started coming out of the buildings. Our men are telling them what's happened."

"Any reactions?" asked the Admiral.

The Captain turned to him and smiled. "They seem relieved!" he said.

The others in the shuttle laughed.

"It's time for me to get to the Palace," said Henry and picked up the metal case.

The Admiral gestured at the armed troops who

walked out of the shuttle. Kyle heard the sound of another hatch opening and two ground cars appeared in front of the doorway.

"Let me go out first, Sire," the Admiral said and led the way outside. He stared around the immediate environment and looked back at the pilot with a question in his face.

"No alien life forms detected, sir," said the Captain.

The Admiral nodded and waited for the others to come out.

Henry took a seat in the second car together with Josh, Kyle and Charlie while the Admiral took the leading vehicle with his troops and they began heading for the Palace.

"How strange this is," said Henry. "I know I have never been here before, but I know it so well. This is my home."

"I hope it's in better shape than the city," said Kyle.

"I imagine the Empress has at least kept her own place in luxury," said Charlie. Her tone was sarcastic. The other men grinned at her.

A low rumble like a distant storm ran around the city. It seemed to vibrate even the ground under their feet.

"What on earth is that?" said Josh, puzzled. "The weather forecast said nothing about thunderstorms."

"They must be wrong," said Charlie. "The sky is getting dark."

They looked up at the sky as what appeared to be a major thunder storm was brewing.

"That's no ordinary storm," said Josh. "The sky is green!"

He was right. The sky had turned a sickly green colour while around it streamers of red raced from horizon to horizon and massive lightning strikes hit the ground in all direction.

At the same time, the ground shook and one or two buildings ahead of them seemed to wave like trees in a wind.

"This isn't an earthquake zone," called Kyle, barely heard above the howling wind that had sprung up and the crack of the lightning bolts. "What's going on?"

"The box!" shouted Henry in panic. "It's burning hot."

"Out!" commanded Kyle. "Something dangerous is happening."

They hurriedly left the car, not before Kyle saw the box containing the Star glowing bright red with huge surges of energy.

The car ahead had also stopped and the four armed men surrounded Henry to protect him.

The storm increased in intensity. There was no rain, but massive bolts of energy thundered to the ground, mostly aimed at the Palace. The building began to glow with an eerie yellow light until the whole Palace was covered.

"That looks like a force field," said Kyle.

A titanic explosion went off some way above them and a thunderbolt struck the ground just a hundred metres away shook the ground. All of them were blown off their feet and for a moment they were unable to breathe as the explosion had blasted all the air away. New air rushed in, making a small typhoon that blew them around like dolls for a second or two before subsiding.

The soldiers gathered round Henry, weapons ready, but there was no sign of hostile forces.

Kyle jumped to his feet, checked Henry first and then with huge relief saw that everybody was safe. He helped Charlie to her feet and she smiled at him.

"I'm fine," she said.

That lifted his spirits and he looked out to the Palace.

"That's still standing," he said.

But even as he said it, a monstrous bolt of lightning struck the Palace and the yellow glow faded. Within seconds the storm faded and the sky cleared.

"What the...? muttered Kyle. He looked back into the car and saw that the metal box appeared to have returned to normal. In sudden fear, he opened it and stared down at the Star. It appeared to be glowing a lot more brightly than before and it was humming loudly. He realised Henry was standing next to him.

"It seems okay," Kyle said and saw that Henry was smiling.

"It should be," Henry said. "It's won."

Before Kyle could ask what he meant by that, the Admiral spoke.

"We have to get to the Palace," he said. "The troops there say we have to see something. They seem very excited."

A few moments later, they entered the Palace grounds through a massive gate that had been opened by the troops. The cars stopped before the main entrance at the base of a flight of stone steps and the occupants got out.

"I'll carry the Star," said Henry and pulled the box out of the car. He refused Kyle's offer to carry it and advanced on the steps. "I remember this so well," he said. "We came out this way for my Coronation."

Admiral Bradshaw approached him, walking rapidly.

"Sire, we have to get to the Chamber of the Star," said the Admiral. "I have no idea where that is."

"This way," replied Henry with a broad smile and led the way along several corridors, walking with confidence. He stopped before a massive door at least three metres high and looking as solid as a bank vault.

"The royal quarters," he said and pointed down to a doorway at the end of one such corridor. "My apartment," he said and pointed at the huge door next to them. "This is where the Star is kept."

He touched the door which swung open soundlessly. Inside was a block of black basalt about a metre on all sides. Several armed men stood along the walls of the room, but what held everybody's attention was the basalt block and what lay on it.

It looked like shards of black glass.

"It's the Dark Star," said Henry. "I think that storm was the two Stars fighting it out."

"It shattered when that huge bolt hit the Palace," said a young officer in combat gear, one of those in the room. "And the storm stopped at just that moment."

Henry put the metal box down on the floor, opened it and raised the Star. There was a gasp of awe from the troops in the chamber. A Star had been part of Yshan legends for five thousand years and few people ever saw it. The last time one had been seen by the people was at Henry's Coronation over a hundred and twenty years before and then it had died.

"Can somebody clean that up?" Henry asked.

Several people, including Josh and Kyle and the troopers began picking up the shards of black glass or just brushing them to the floor with their arms until the surface was clear.

Henry placed the Star on the basalt block and stood back.

"About time," he said. "I'm sorry it took so long but we'll start clearing up right away."

He turned away and left the Chamber, followed by the rest and the door swung closed behind the last soldier to leave.

"It's safe," he said in reply to the Admiral's unspoken question. "The Star knows who to let in and who to keep out. Now, let's see who's in my apartment."

He began to walk down to the far door with Josh, Charlie and Kyle beside him, but he didn't have to move far because the door opened and a figure emerged.

Kyle's first reaction was admiration. The woman was quite beautiful, a pale, aristocratic face with long black hair down her back. She wore a stylish white dress with no ornamentation at all.

She stared at the group watching her and Kyle changed his views about her beauty. There was a mean, ugly look about her, an air of barely suppressed fury. She stared at each of the group in turn, her gaze passing over the soldiers and the Admiral without interest, but her glare at Charlie was intense before passing onto Josh. Then she gasped in amazement and went white.

"Josh?" she whispered, shock in her face. "How can this be?" Her gaze moved onto Kyle and this time the shock made her stumble. "This isn't possible," she mumbled as if her mouth had frozen. "My brother died many years ago. You too, Josh, you cannot be here. This is impossible."

"And do you remember me, Sophie?" said Henry softly.

The Empress Sophie stared at him, her eyes widened even more and then she collapsed to the floor.

* * *

"Quite a severe shock, but I've given her a sedative," said the doctor. "She'll be fine, Sire."

"Thank you, doctor but stay with us, please," replied Henry.

The doctor nodded and retreated to the back of the room.

They were in what had been Henry's personal apartment until it had been taken over by Sophie after she had been installed as Empress. Sophie sat, half lying in one armchair while Henry, Kyle, Charlie and Josh sat in a half circle around her. The Admiral sat at the back of the room and several armed guards remained outside in case of any surprises.

The silence lasted another two or three minutes while they waited for Sophie to recover. Over an hour had passed since her collapse into a dead faint and Kyle had already thought that she was looking older than when she had first appeared.

Sophie stirred and sat up. She took a few deep breaths before looking up at the others watching her.

"Kyle, it *can't* be you," she whispered.

Kyle looked calmly back at her. "Quite correct, Sophie. Your brother was my great grandfather."

"But you look so like him," she continued, her voice low and croaky. "You too, Josh, you haven't changed at all," she added.

"Several generations have passed," said Josh. "But you seem to have stayed young."

Sophie didn't seem to hear him. She was staring at Charlie. She seemed also to be deliberately ignoring Henry.

"Who's this?" she demanded.

Charlie gave a small, cold smile. "Who else could I be but Charlie?" she replied.

"At least you don't look like her," said Sophie.

"We're not related," said Charlie.

Sophie sat up straight. Kyle was sure of it now, she was looking a lot older than a couple of hours ago.

"I demand to see my Uncle Omaron," she said, struggling to put authority into her words.

"Difficult," replied Kyle. "Omaron is in a cell back on the new capital world. He's aging very fast and not likely to last much longer."

Sophie's eyes widened in fear. "He's... aging?" she whispered.

"As are you, Sophie," said Kyle deliberately.

Sophie gasped as if in pain. She jumped to her feet and ran to a full-length mirror on one wall. When she saw her image, she let out a small scream and put her hands to her face.

"This can't be," she rasped. "The Star promised..."

"Your Dark Star is dead, Sophie," said Henry.

"Yshan has a new Star, your allies have been destroyed. This is the end for you."

Slowly, Sophie walked back to her seat and almost fell into it. Kyle was certain of it now, she had aged at least twenty years in the last hour. Her hair no longer had the perfect sheen of youth and her complexion was developing lines that had not been there before.

Finally, she looked at Henry.

"I don't understand," she whispered. "The Emperor had no family, how could you be descended from him?"

"I'm not. I'm the original."

She shook her head in bewilderment. "No, that's not possible, I...."

"You killed me?" said Henry softly. "Yes, you did, cousin Sophie."

"Then how...?"

"The Golden Mask. Remember the Golden Mask? Nobody ever understood that strange ceremony of having the mask take the shape of the new Emperor's face. But it took my cells, my memories and it stayed in touch with my mind to make a new copy of me. Do you know I'm only three years old? But I have every memory right up to my death, including meeting you on Earth the first time, how I beat you at chess and how you threw such a tantrum because of it."

Sophie's face was white and she looked ill.

"What now?" she managed to say.

"The Yshan people have suffered for over a

century under your appalling rule," said Henry. "They need to see that it's over."

He beckoned the young officer with the troops.

"Take Princess Sophie Yshan into custody," he said. "Lead her outside and place her in an open vehicle and drive her slowly to the military headquarters, if that still exists."

"It does, Sire. We checked," replied the officer.

"Good," said Henry. "Make it a long, circuitous trip so as many people as possible get to see her. Arrange a press conference for all media and announce that the Princess will stand trial for treason. Keep her in a cell there, show scenes of her on the media frequently. She gets no special treatment, no extra comforts, no food other than regular prisoners' rations. The people will see her as nothing but a common criminal. I'm sure that will please them and convince them that a new life is starting for them."

The young man moved over to Sophie and held her arm, making her stand up. He waved over two soldiers and they held her up as they led her out of the room. She seemed stooped, not the slender, erect young woman they had met such a short time ago.

"I don't think she'll last long enough for a trial," said Josh.

"Probably not," agreed Henry. "But the important thing is that the people see her arrested, in prison and nothing like the beautiful Empress of the last century of so."

"That sounds good," said Kyle.

Henry grinned like a little boy then turned to the Admiral.

"Admiral," he said. "We need to start rebuilding. We need an interim civilian government until elections can be held. I want you to arrange huge food supplies from our previous home and get engineers, medical people, teachers, everything we need to rebuild our civilisation..."

The two men moved away and out of earshot and the room gradually cleared as everybody began their new duties.

Charlie turned to Josh, a small flush on her face. "Little brother, can't you find things to do somewhere else?"

Josh looked at her and smiled. "I'm sure this heroic Fleet Pilot can find work out there," he said and waved cheerfully at the other two as he walked out.

Charlie and Kyle looked at each other.

"You're a very impressive Ship's Captain, Commander Yshan," she said.

Kyle grinned, feeling like a schoolboy. "Aw, shucks, Ma'am," he said. "I bet you say that to all the steely-eyed, heroic ship's captains who have just saved the Empire."

She chuckled. "All of them," she said and touched his hand.

"I think we deserve a holiday," Kyle said.

"I most enthusiastically agree," Charlotte replied.

Chapter 45 – A Grand Finale

The wedding of Captain Kyle Yshan, Duke of the Moidari Sector, Guardian of the Six Home Planets and newly assigned to the Captaincy of the Battle Cruiser, *"Admiral Sestucal,"* flagship of the Yshan Galactic Fleet, to Charlotte Foster Bradshaw, only daughter of Joshua and Eleanor Bradshaw was truly a grand affair.

The ceremony took place in the Royal Palace on the Home World of Yshan and was attended by dignitaries from over two hundred planets within the Yshan Empire extending over two Galaxies, as well as the officers and men and women of the frigate, *"Charlie Foster,"* the previous command of Kyle Yshan. They were all in their "Ceremonial Whites," beautifully cut white tunics, black belts and officer-pattern swords with gold handles and their names engraved on the blades.

Also in attendance was His Imperial Majesty, Garamax the Nineteenth, Seventy-Second Emperor of the Yshan Galactic Empire. He sat in the front row with Charlotte's parents, dressed simply in a smart suit so as not to distract attention from the bridal couple.

Standing next to the groom as Best Man was Lieutenant-Commander Joshua Bradshaw, brother of the bride and grandson of the Fleet Commander, newly promoted and also assigned as Tactical Officer to the flagship Battle Cruiser in the Yshan Imperial Galactic Fleet.

When the ceremony had been completed by Fleet Admiral Joshua Bradshaw, Commander of the Twelve Sectors of the Galactic Fleet, the Best Man drew his sword and joined the other fleet personnel to form two lines holding their swords high, tips touching in the middle making a grand archway for the newly married couple to walk through.

The bride looked quite stunning and her parents both had tears running down their cheeks as she walked past them giving a beautiful smile in their direction.

The Empire's media made much of the fact that the last royal wedding had also been that of Charlotte to Kyle over a hundred and thirty years ago and the populations of the many planets throughout the Empire seemed delighted at this evidence of the restoration of old traditions.

The convoy of vehicles carrying the wedding party drove through the city streets, heavily lined with delighted observers and back to the Royal Palace for the private reception with the Emperor.

These proceedings were relaxed and informal but when Kyle saw a young officer enter the room and approach the Emperor, he sensed something critical had happened. The man spoke briefly to Henry then walked out. Henry saw Kyle observing the meeting and nodded at him, pointing briefly at Charlie and the Admiral, both of whom were engaged in cheerful conversations with others.

Kyle moved over to them and touched their shoulders and they followed him to join Henry.

"I just got the news," Henry said, some sadness in his face. "Both Sophie and Omaron died just minutes ago. The doctors say they collapsed and they resembled very, very old people at that moment."

"The last direct link with the Old Empire, barring yourself," said the Admiral.

"Indeed," said Henry with a nod. "Let's make sure this one stays peaceful until it's our turn to move on."

"Do you think that one day, we Yshans will be part of a new Star that we give to the next people to take over our world?" asked Charlie.

"Without a doubt," said Henry. "Now let's get back to the party. We have a new Empire to celebrate."

** The End ""